After Dark

Nightfall Book Two

Jeffery Martin
Botzenhart

Solstice Publishing - www.solsticepublishing.com

Nightfall – Book Two

After Dark

By

Jeffery Martin Botzenhart

Dedication:

To my sons, Dylan, Owen, and Ethan…my best friends!

Part One

By the Light of the Moon

Chapter One

Mesmerized by the fluid motions of the flames, Sebastian reached out with his trembling hands, feeling the fire's warmth radiating to his chilled fingers. "I think it's getting colder," he uttered, watching the fog from his breath evaporate before his eyes. Inhaling, he smelled the stench of smoke rising from the charred wood, which was surprising since his sense of smell had mostly left him.

Poking a long stick into the blisteringly hot embers, his dad smiled, then commenting, "I remember when late summer still meant warm weather." He held a mug out to Sebastian, "Here kiddo, have some more hot chocolate."

After taking it from his dad, Sebastian raised the rim of the mug to his lips, spilling some down his chin when sipping it.

"Do you want me to hold that for you?"

"No," Sebastian quietly answered. "I can manage."

A strong gust of wind disturbed the branches of the trees surrounding their camp site. Leaves wrenched from the trees scattered around them. Glancing up, Sebastian gazed upon the vastness of the night sky full of brilliant stars. He also noticed how some of the tree limbs appeared to softly glow in the dark, lit by the light of the moon.

Static from his dad's old battery-powered radio drew his attention away from their surroundings. While he was adjusting the dial, every so often a word or two could be heard. But without a clear signal here in the mountains of Maine, picking up a channel for more than a few seconds proved impossible. "Are you trying to find some music?"

"That would be nice," his dad answered.

"Who were we listening to at the lighthouse?"

"Journey, they were a classic rock group. I've been listening to them since I was a kid."

Sighing with frustration, his dad turned off the radio, setting it down next to his backpack.

"You should try to get some sleep. We're about twenty miles or so from the Canadian border. It's going to be a long walk."

Setting his mug aside, Sebastian crawled into his sleeping bag without pulling the zipper up and keeping his head and shoulders out from under the fabric. Reminded of how it felt when he was hidden inside the black body bag dumped into San Francisco Bay, the thought of being too confined frightened him. For the first time in hours, though, he grinned when his dad stepped over and knelt next to him. He tucked the lower part of the sleeping bag under him, as Sebastian commented, "I think I'm too old for that."

"Luckily for you, I'm not too old to do it," his dad smiled and then leaned down, kissing his forehead. "Good night, kiddo. I love you."

"I love you, too, Dad." Slowly exhaling, Sebastian closed his eyes, listening to the sounds of his dad slipping into his own sleeping bag and the wood crackling as it burned. Just as he felt himself drifting off to sleep, the echoing hoot of an owl called out to the night. He wondered what it was saying and who to. Nestling his chin against his red hoodie, he thought about this for a short while before dreamlessly dozing off.

***

Annoyed by chirping birds, Lee rolled over, breathing in the light scent from the fire that burned out sometime during the night. Chilled by the morning air, he pulled his sleeping bag tighter against him before opening his eyes. He held still when looking across the way to his still sleeping son. Next to Sebastian lay a large German shepherd, its brown eyes tranquilly gazing out while nestling its snout on his chest. The dog shifted his head toward Sebastian and began licking his cheek, waking him.

Sebastian stretched groggily and sat up, rubbing the sleep from his eyes before saying to the animal "Where did you come from?"

The shepherd wagged its tail while nudging his hand.

"I think it wants you to pet it," Lee said with a grin. Slowly reaching his hand down, Sebastian ran his fingers through the dog's soft coat, its tail wagging excitedly.

"I wonder what his name is?" Sebastian asked, searching the collar for a tag.

"Silas," a man's frail voice answered. Quickly rising to his feet, Lee grabbed for his fire-poking stick, ready to defend themselves. While the dog pawed at Sebastian's jeans, obviously wanting to be petted again, an elderly man appeared through some high bushes. "Please put the stick down, I mean you no harm," he offered. Wearing a derby cap and black-and-red-plaid jacket, the man removed a pipe from his mouth and extended his other hand to Lee. "The name's Thomas Lesterman, and who might you be?"

Guardedly completing their handshake, Lee answered, "I'm Lee. This is my son Sebastian."

Quietly looking them over for a moment, Thomas asked, "Would you gentlemen care for some breakfast?" The noticeable contractions from Sebastian's stomach answered well enough, with Thomas wryly grinning. "Come on, the house is just at the bottom of the hill."

After rolling their sleeping bags and gathering their things, Lee and Sebastian followed Thomas down a partially-stoned path leading through the woods. Silas remained at Sebastian's side, thoroughly enjoying the constant petting he received. Emerging through the tree line, across a sloped field of tall grass swayed by a mountain breeze, they saw an old stone farmhouse with faded red shutters and a white-painted barn in need of a fresh coat of paint. Plumes of smoke escaping from the chimney seemed to disappear as shafts of morning sunlight pierced through the tree branches. When glancing toward the house, Lee noticed someone staring out a window on the second floor. Drawing his eyes away in watching Sebastian and the dog, when he looked back up to the window, the person was gone.

Before entering the house, Thomas turned to them. "If you don't mind, my wife would appreciate it if you both removed your shoes before coming inside. She just *hates* scuff marks on her wooden floors." Smiling kindly at them, Lee and Sebastian took off their shoes and followed him inside.

Lee breathed in the pleasant aromas of brewed coffee and cooked bacon while Thomas walked up behind his wife who was preoccupied with taking freshly-baked biscuits out of a white vintage oven. "Ma, we've got company," the old man said, placing his hand on her shoulder.

Quickly turning, a smile burst across her face when looking at Sebastian and hardly noticing Lee standing there. "Hello," she greeted cheerfully.

"Ma, this is Sebastian and his father, Lee. Gentlemen, this is Constance."

Now taking notice of Lee, her greeting sounded blatantly hesitant. "Good morning," she said while not fully addressing him. Both Lee and Sebastian exchanged curious glances as Thomas motioned for them to sit at the farmhouse table.

Lee glanced around, appreciating the home's distinctive charm, from the unique wooden cabinetry and overhead beams to the river-stone fireplace and antique furnishings. Yet something inside him caused him to feel tense about Constance's continuing glances toward Sebastian. Maybe he was just being overprotective, but her reaction to his son unnerved him. Short in stature, her white hair and white apron, worn over a blue floral dress, presented a grandmotherly appearance. But that was where the comparison ended. While he couldn't quite put his finger on what it was that bothered him he continued to watch her with growing unease. Thomas's words, however, lured his attention from her. "I'm sorry?" Lee said.

"I asked where you and your son are heading."

"Montreal; we're meeting a relative there," he lied.

Appearing thoughtful for a moment, Thomas then responded, "I hear the Canadians are turning people away from the border. They've even blocked some of the bridges to restrict entry."

"Why?"

"Since the New England states have voted to separate from the Union, Washington is putting pressure of Canada and other countries not to recognize our break-away region or take in any refugees."

"I see," Lee mumbled.

"You don't have a car," Thomas commented.

"We ran out of gas ten miles south of here," Lee said. "Every time we tried to refill the tank we were turned away."

"That's because the government blockaded the coast and closed the New York border to all shipments, everything from oil and gas to food. With winter just a few months away, I imagine they believe starving us and keeping us cold will force New England to stay in the Union."

"Enough with all that *terrible* nonsense," Constance admonished her husband. "You'll frighten him." Fixing her eyes on Sebastian, she asked in the manner one might speak to a toddler, "Would you care for some breakfast, Ben?"

Looking sideways to his dad, he hesitantly responded, "My name is Sebastian and—yes ma'am, I would like some breakfast." Beaming a smile, Constance took the top plate from a stack of four and served him bacon, biscuits, and scrambled eggs. Rising from her seat, she carried the plate over to him, setting it down in front of him and also placing a napkin over his lap. "Thank you," Sebastian said, staring somewhat away. Covering his mouth with his hand, Lee tried to contain his amusement as Constance doted over his son, with Sebastian clearly stunned. Thomas filled his plate with food, seeming oblivious to his wife treating a teenage boy as if he a four-year-old.

As Constance sat down, Sebastian was about to take a bite of his eggs when she stopped him. "*Someone* has forgotten his table manners," She said, staring at him.

Now looking fully at his dad, both exchanged disturbed glances when she continued, "Ben, will you please lead us in the saying of grace?"

His eyes bulging, Lee interrupted on his son's behalf, "We silently say grace—in having private reflections with God." Appearing at first unsettled by his answer, she composed herself and began eating, saying nothing further yet keeping a close eye on Sebastian.

Later, as they were finishing eating breakfast, they heard the sound of thunder in the distance. Sneaking a look to Sebastian, Lee then turned his attention to Thomas. "We greatly appreciate your hospitality, but should be going. We have a long walk ahead of us."

"*Nonsense!*" Constance burst out before her husband could say anything. "There's a storm coming. Both of you will be staying with us until it passed, at *least* for one night."

"That's very kind of you, but we are expected in Montreal—."

Cutting off his words with her voice raised, she insisted, "Not another word. You will be staying with us tonight and that—is—that." Motioning across the table, she continued, "Why just *look* at how Ben's hands are shaking. You've frightened him in wanting to go out into a coming storm. Shame on you!"

Barely glancing up from his plate, Thomas added, "I wouldn't argue the point if I were you."

Releasing a sigh, Lee uttered, "Well then, once more, we accept your gracious hospitality." And when certain that Thomas and his wife were looking away, Lee winked and shook his head to Sebastian, silently letting him know they would not be staying.

Chapter Two

Climbing the steps to the second floor, with Silas staying close to Sebastian, Thomas led them to the first door. "Lee, this is your room for the night." Turning toward Sebastian, he said, "Young man, follow me." Walking farther down to the end of the hallway, Thomas extended his arm. "This will be your room." Then pointing to a door opposite this, he added while looking at Lee, "The bathroom is here. You'll probably feel better after a nice hot shower." Looking once more at Sebastian, he urged, "Go *in* and make yourself comfortable."

Doing as he was told, he and Silas slowly walked into the bedroom with the old man closing the door behind them.

After climbing up to the foot of the bed, the dog laid down, its eyes not leaving sight of Sebastian. Petting his new friend, he then wandered over to a dresser next to the door. Framed photographs of the old couple, showing warm smiles with a boy his age, were displayed amidst a few baseball trophies and two plastic models of hot rods. A brief thought crossed his mind, wondering both where the boy was and how long ago this photograph had been taken.

Hearing the sounds of the shower running, his heart sank in realizing his dad changed his mind and that they *would* be spending the night. He wished they'd never agreed to come here with the old man, although he liked having the company of his dog. Maybe after his dad finished showering, he could convince him to leave.

While backing away, something in the corner or the room caught his interest. Finding his glasses from his backpack, he put them on so he could read the titles of numerous books, neatly arranged on a floor-to-ceiling shelf. Recognizing many of the titles reminded him of his book collection, left behind in San Francisco. One title, unfamiliar to him, piqued his interest. As he was just opening the cover, there was a faint tap at his door.

Holding his breath, his heart beat rapidly when the door quietly opened. Sebastian exhaled with relief when he saw his dad leaning in from the hallway. At first he was confused, seeing his dad fully dressed while the shower was running. Closing it behind him, Lee wrapped him in his strong embrace. "I'm sorry if I scared you, kiddo." Drawing back, Sebastian noticed a strange look from his dad.

"What?"

"Nothing, just never seen you wearing glasses before." Smiling, he added, "They look good on you."

"I thought you were taking a shower?"

"That's what I want them to think. I don't want them to know we're talking."

Growing nervous, Sebastian blurted out, "Dad, I don't want to stay here. There's something about these people that scares me."

"I know what you mean, kiddo. There's something going on here that I can't put my finger on. Heck, the old lady can't even get your name right," Lee lightly commented, trying to get Sebastian to smile.

Reaching over, Sebastian retrieved one of the photographs from the top of the dresser. Handing it to his dad, he whispered, "That's Ben."

Studying the photograph of Thomas, his wife, and their son, Lee faintly read the words decorating the birthday cake in front of them, *"Happy 16th birthday Ben."* Returning it to Sebastian, Lee uttered, "That's it. We gotta get out of here as soon as we can."

"How are we gonna get away from them?"

"I don't know, yet. Maybe, sneak out after dark—but I'd rather leave sooner."

"Dad, I don't want to stay that long. Can't we just go now?" A blinding flash of lightning, followed by a strong clap of thunder, seemed to offer an answer to his question. Moving over to the window, they both looked out as driving sheets of rain pelted the glass. Sighing, Sebastian mumbled, "I guess we'll have to wait until after the storm's over."

"No," Lee whispered. "This is probably the best time to leave." As soon as he said this, creaking sounds from the staircase alerted them that someone was coming upstairs. Backing over to the closet, Lee hid himself inside, keeping the door slightly ajar.

After a soft knock the bedroom door opened, and standing in the doorway was the old lady. "I wanted to check on you, to make sure you're comfortable?" she fretted.

"Yes, ma'am. The room is really nice. Thank you," he politely answered.

Noticing the book in his hand, she anxiously asked, "Do you like to read?"

"Yes, ma'am."

"Do you have a favorite author?"

Swallowing hard, he answered, "Charles Dickens."

"*How lovely!*" she gushed at his response. Appearing confused, Constance continued, "Do you remember when I used to read *A Christmas Carol* to you?"

Feeling a chill run down his spine, Sebastian forced out a lie, "Yes, ma'am." This answer only seemed to confuse her further. Remembering the other photograph of her and her son baking cookies, thinking fast in wanting to get rid of her, he asked, "Do you still have the recipe for the cookies we used to bake together?"

Her jaw quivered as it appeared she was trying to recall this memory. And then brightness returned to her expression. "We should bake some cookies!" she exclaimed.

Keeping his lie going, he suggested, "Maybe you could make them for me? I'd like to read for a little while, if you don't mind."

"Not at all," Constance replied, her eyes glazed over as if she'd been hypnotized. "You go right ahead and read. And later I'll bring you some cookies and a nice tall glass of milk." There was spryness to her steps as she rushed away.

Closing the door behind her, Sebastian began hyperventilating from fear as his dad emerged from the closet. Hugging him close, his dad whispered in his ear, "That was brilliant, kiddo. I'm so proud of you."

"*Please*, can we get out of here," Sebastian mumbled, nearly in tears.

Kissing his forehead while holding back his own tears, Lee answered, "Come on, we're leaving."

Before they could take a step, there was a series of loud thump against the ceiling, sounding as if something in the above attic was being moved, like someone rolling around on the floor. "Whats going on up there?" Lee mumbled.

"Dad, let's just go, *please*," Sebastian begged.

Nodding his head while caressing his son's cheek, Lee stepped out of the bedroom first with Sebastian and Silas following close. Once out in the hallway, they both heard Thomas's painful moans, coming through the open attic door behind them.

Intending to ignore this, their escape came to a halt when hearing the old woman climbing the steps. Returning to the bedroom, Lee pointed for Sebastian to lie on the bed while he hid again in the closet. With the dog snuggling up close to him, Sebastian wondered if Silas knew what they were doing and was somehow offering his help in deceiving the old woman. When Constance entered the room without knocking, Sebastian hoped to convince her he'd fallen asleep. Hearing her lightly treading around the bed, he then felt his glasses being pulled off his face before she kissed him on the cheek. "Sweet dreams, my precious Ben," she faintly whispered and then quietly left.

Feeling his pulse racing with his chest heaving, Sebastian rapidly sat up. Looking at the dog eagerly wagging its tail, he reached over to pet it. "Good boy," he whispered.

"Both of you were awesome," Lee added, also petting Silas. "Come on," he urged. We need to get out of here." This time after stepping out into the hallway, the bedroom door inexplicably locked behind them. "It will be okay," Lee said. But just as before, their escape came to a halt when they heard her climbing the stairs again. With his dad waving his arm, Sebastian understood that he wanted them to climb a few steps on the dark staircase leading up to the attic, pulling the door almost closed to spy out down the hallway.

"Thomas, Thomas!" she called out. "There's a strange man at the door. I don't want to let him in." Spying over his dad's shoulder, Sebastian noticed how confused the old woman was again. For a moment Constance stood there, appearing lost, before heading back downstairs.

Just as they were about to leave, they both heard Thomas's moans coming from up in the attic. Silas growled while glancing in that direction, almost as if warning them. Noticing the dim light above, Lee pointed up and passed by Sebastian, climbing until he reached the last step. He then stood up and disappeared from sight.

Anxious in being left alone, Sebastian followed his dad up to the attic. With Silas staying close to him, after stepping away from the dark stairwell, he saw his dad kneeling down next to Thomas. He also saw a police officer, bound with ropes to a chair. Sebastian instantly recognized him, the Lesterman's son, Ben. Cautiously moving closer, he read the name on his badge, "Officer Bentley T Lesterman, Boston PD."

Leaning with his back resting against an old trunk, Thomas wheezed through his blood-covered face, "That's not my son. It's just a machine." Sebastian and his dad exchanged stunned expressions as the old man spoke further, "After losing contact with Ben, we went to Boston to find out why he wasn't returning our calls and letters. All we found was *that—thing*. I think they call it a *replicate*."

"So—you never found your real son?" Lee asked.

"No." Blankly staring out, he added, "Constance was grief-stricken, just drove her over the edge. She insisted we bring that thing home with us. I had a devil of a time trying to get that thing in the car. But there were some protesters who beat it to the ground, causing enough damage to make it easier for me. Somehow, in her mind, this was supposed to replace Ben. But it's just a machine, one meant to harm people, a weapon, nothing more."

Stepping around behind the replicate, Sebastian discovered the back of its head missing, with the internal robotics completely exposed. "Dad, he's right," Sebastian mumbled, both frightened and shocked. His fear grew worse with thunder closely sounding out and seeing brief flashes of lightning through the small attic windows.

Adding to his confession, Thomas revealed, "I came up here to set it free, now that we have a replacement for Ben," nodding his head in Sebastian's direction. Glancing at Lee, he finished, "I was going to kill you while you slept and keep your boy." A rush of air then left Thomas's lungs, with his body convulsing and his eyes solidly fixed on Sebastian. Reaching his arm out, as if begging for help, his silent plea was ignored when Lee stood up, stepping away from him. A moment later, his hand dropped with his body growing limp.

Chapter Three

Pulling Sebastian to him, Lee cradled his son's frightened face in his hands. Speaking calmly, he whispered, "We gotta get out of here, as far away as we can." Silently nodding his head, Sebastian started to glance down at Thomas's dead body but his dad eased his chin up. "No, he's not worth looking at."

Returning to the upstairs hallway, Lee placed a finger to his lips as they tip-toed passed the bathroom and bedroom doors before reaching the staircase. Spying through the white spindles, they could hear the old woman talking to someone downstairs. Her voice sounded distressed, but considering her current state of mind, this was expected. With each step descended, her tone grew louder and more shrilled. Stopping for a second, they tried to listen to what she was saying. Her hysterics, however, made each word seem like nonsense. Just as they reached the bottom, a loud echoing gun blast made them jump.

An eerie silence gripped the house, with only the sounds of rain and rolling thunder from outside competing with the droning ticks from the hands of a wall-mounted clock. Deeply exhaling, Lee motioned for Sebastian to follow him. Peering through the doorway into the kitchen, both saw Constance holding a shotgun as she stood there, looking outside with the screen door flapping in the stormy wind.

Creeping up behind her, Lee halted reaching out for the gun when she dropped it and then staggered back, falling onto the seat of a chair. Cautiously moving up next to her, they stopped walking when she vacantly glanced over at Sebastian. "I'm sorry Ben, I might have burned the cookies. I smell smoke."

Swallowing hard while feeling sick to his stomach, Sebastian uttered, "It's okay. I wasn't hungry."

"Where are you going?" she asked, her eyes wandering in all directions.

"I'm going out to play."

"Isn't it raining outside?"

With thunder loudly following a burst of lightning, he lied, "No, I think it stopped."

Wrapping his arm across his son's chest, Lee pulled him away from her, both backing out onto the porch. Turning around, they instantly frozen, seeing a man dressed in black, lying on the ground. Constance was right. She was, in fact smelling smoke, not from burning cookies in the oven but instead rising from the robotics within the man's replicate head.

Noticing a black sedan parked in the driveway, Lee mumbled, "Damn."

"What?"

"They followed us," Lee answered.

"Who?" Sebastian breathlessly asked.

Sighing, Lee revealed, "That's a Dryden company car. I can tell by the design on the license plate. *Somehow* they tracked us here. But *how*?"

With a memory flashing in his mind, Sebastian closed his eyes for a moment before reaching into the bottom of his backpack. His hand trembling uncontrollably, he pulled out an old cell phone, and handed it to his dad.

"What's this?"

With tears streaming down his face, Sebastian choked out, "I'm sorry."

Dragging him close, Lee kept whispering, "It's okay; it's okay."

Wiping his tears away, Sebastian revealed, "Scotty placed this in my backpack, so that he could find me. I guess I never thought about taking it out."

"They must have hacked into it and tracked us here."

"Do you think Scotty's okay?" Sebastian blurted.

Attempting to ease his fears, Lee slightly grinned. "Knowing how careful Abdul is, I'm certain he would have made Scotty leave everything traceable behind in San Francisco." Studying the cell phone, he added, "I think we can buy ourselves a little time with this, at least enough to reach the Canadian border."

"How?"

Thinking for a moment, Lee then answered, "I can program the car to return to where it was sent from, probably Portland or Boston. But, I'm going to have to ask you to do something."

"What?" Sebastian asked, feeling his pulse racing with panic.

"Listen to me. The car over there has life sensors built into it. It can tell if the person inside is alive. *That's* what the replicate was sent here for, to bring a *live* person back. *Me,* I'm guessing. They've known all along that neither of us are dead and that we'd find each other. I was sure of it back at the lighthouse. By using this phone, they found us. Let's send it back to them, along with a live person." Motioning with his head toward the house, he continued, "We can send them, her. That's where I need your help. She won't come outside for me but I think she will for you."

After they pulled on their shoes, Lee stepped into the pouring rain, lugging the replicate through the mud to its car. Looking then back to Sebastian, he reassuringly nodded his head, silently urging him on.

Taking a deep breath, Sebastian griped the door handle with his trembling hand while summoning the courage to step inside the house. With his breathing shallow, he pulled open the door and walked into the kitchen. Constance looked up from her seat. "*Mom*," he barely mumbled while closing his eyes. Swallowing hard, he spoke in a louder voice, "Mom."

"Yes, Ben, dear," she answered, a smile creeping across her face.

With thoughts rapidly passing through his mind, he remembered the photographs in Ben's room. "Mom, you forgot that today's my birthday."

"Oh, my lord!" she said, drawing her hands up to her face. "How could I have forgotten such a thing?"

Forcing calmness to his tone, Sebastian asked, "Can we go to the store to get my present?"

"Oh, my, yes! What would you like, my dear?"

Thinking clear, he answered, "How 'bout a book? Maybe one by Charles Dickens."

"That would be lovely," Constance answered, her eyes turning blank while looking away.

"Can we leave now?"

"Of course! Find your father so we can go."

Sebastian jumped aside, startled when the screen door opened. Reaching his arm in, Lee grabbed hold of a set of car keys hanging on a hook next to a wall-mounted telephone. Nodding his head with encouragement, he waved for Sebastian to lead her outside.

Once out on the porch, she blankly asked, "Ben, where's your father."

"He's waiting in the car."

"Oh, *that* man, always so impatient." Stepping into the rain, she commented, "It's a shame that it's raining on your birthday." Sebastian didn't reply as he led her to the car. After helping her into the passenger-side front seat, he closed the door, breathing out a deep exhale of relief. Lee pressed a button on the dashboard, starting the car engine before closing the driver's door. The car backed down the driveway and sped away on the country road.

Turning and doubling over, Sebastian began heaving into the grass until there was nothing left in his stomach. Shaking with chills, he sluggishly stood up, closing his eyes until the nauseous sensation in him subsided. Feeling completely drained of his energy, he could barely turn around to face his dad.

Now fully drenched by the unyielding rainfall, Lee and Sebastian stood apart from each other near Thomas's old pickup truck. Clearly expressing guilt and sadness on his face, his dad uttered, "I'm sorry, kiddo." At this moment, Sebastian understood how his dad's strength and resolve in protecting him could falter. He could see how much it broke his heart to endure these final minutes at the Lesterman farm. But there really was no other way.

Trying to find his inner strength, Sebastian responded, "I love you, Dad." Lee stepped over and they held on to each other, pressing their foreheads together. "I'd do it again, if you ask me to."

"I don't think I could."

Meeting him eye-to-eye, Sebastian remarked, "You may have to. We both know it."

Appearing unsure of what else to say, Lee nodded his head with reluctant agreement over this. Finding his voice again after a few seconds, he mumbled, "Come on, kiddo."

***

Although the thunder and lightning had stopped, the rain continued falling steadily against the windshield. Sebastian's eyes kept focus on the wipers, mindlessly counting off as they passed before his view of the lonely road ahead. The warmth seeping through the truck's air vents did little to calm the chills gripping his body. Reaching over, his dad pulled a blanket closer to

Sebastian's neck, then tenderly ran the back of his hand over his son's cheek. Curled up between them, Silas's ears perked up a little when Lee traced his fingers through the fur on his head, resting in Sebastian's lap.

Farther down the road, seeing the blinking light of a roadside diner, Lee said, "I'm going to stop for some coffee. Are you hungry?"

"I don't know," Sebastian quietly answered.

"You should probably try to eat something."

"Okay."

Once parked with Silas staying in the truck, Sebastian followed his dad into the diner, a long silvery building which looked like a passenger coach from an old train. Finding two seats at the far end of the bar, he sat next to his dad as the waitress approached. "Now, you two look like you've had a rough day. Why just look at how this young man is shaking from being wet and cold. What can I get you, honey?" she asked, kindly then smiling.

"He's not feeling well. I think he'll just have some toast," Lee ordered for him.

"Poor dear," she commented. "And what about you?"

"Just coffee, please."

"Coming right up."

Glancing up at a wall-mounted television, both were drawn to the story the newscaster was presenting. *"Today, the country and world are dealing with the latest release of incriminating information from the so-called Nightfall virus. Damaging evidence suggests more government programs violating public sector privacy and espionage procedures by top foreign affairs officials targeting leaders, this time in the Far East. So far only the governments of Malaysia and Indonesia have confirmed these allegations and are promising swift retribution through the United Nations against members of the previous administration."*

"Turn that off," an old man sitting several stools away barked out at the waitress. Leaning over to another old man sitting next to him, he added with disgust, "A shame they can't stop that information being leaked. It's a good thing they killed the guy who released the secret files. He was a traitor."

From the corner of his eye, Sebastian watched his dad clench his hands, wincing as if the man's words had injured him. Placing his hand upon his dad's shoulder, he caught glimpse of a slight grin while lightly exhaling his frustration.

"Now, Earl, you stop that talk," the waitress scolded the old man. "Just look at how that boy is shaking down there. You're scaring him." Looking at Sebastian, she smiled, "Honey, your toast will be ready soon." Filling his dad's mug with steaming coffee, she left for the kitchen.

Easing his chin onto his folded arms on the counter, without looking at his dad, he faintly asked, "Does it bother you, what that guy said?"

Sighing, Lee quietly answered, "Yeah."

"Why is it called *Nightfall*?"

"Because a lot of people are afraid of the dark. They fear what's hiding in the shadows." After sipping some coffee, he continued, "For the longest time, people were frightened by terrorists and civil unrest brought on by racial and social tensions fueled by hatred. Many willingly turned a blind eye when the government enacted policies they claimed were meant to keep everyone safe, including the use of replicates. And little-by-little people traded away their freedom for a false sense of security. Checks and balances were quietly eliminated as were opponents to the government's plans. The system as a whole lost its sense of transparency. But too many people were late in recognizing what they'd sacrificed. Once the laws and lies were in place, there was to be no stopping them—until I unleashed the truth." Sighing again, he finished, "I just want people to live freely without fear. That's the life I want for you and me. If that makes me a traitor, then so be it."

Chapter Four

Once outside the diner, Sebastian and his dad noticed the rain had stopped, though the low grey clouds overhead appeared as if they could burst again without warning. Stepping over to the truck, Lee opened the door, letting Silas out. "Grab your backpack. We're leaving the truck here," he told Sebastian while looking in both directions down the road.

"How far are we from Canada?" Sebastian asked with Silas nudging his hand in wanting to be petted.

"I'd say roughly a mile, judging from the last sign we passed." Tossing the keys on the seat, Lee closed the door as they started walking away.

Glancing back at the abandoned truck, Sebastian felt some relief in being rid of another reminder of their terrible time at the Lesterman farm. The only remaining reminder, padding between him and his dad, was one he felt he could keep, such was the bond he now had with Silas. Wandering over to the roadside, Sebastian found a branch, which he broke in half. "Here, boy. Fetch!" Tossing the stick ahead of them, the dog bolted to retrieve it. Returning it to his new master, Silas impatiently pranced until Sebastian continued their game. And for the first time since finding his dad at the lighthouse, a sense of peacefulness flooded through him. Not even the tremors coursing through his hands or the stiffness of his muscles could corrupt this moment. He guessed his dad felt the same, with the grin on his bearded face revealing as much.

Yet all moments of peace eventually come to pass. As they continued walking toward the Canadian border, a creeping mist shrouded the road in the direction they were heading. At first, it appeared almost ghost-like. But as they traveled further into it, the denseness rendered the surrounding forest colorless and seemingly robbed the landscape of wildlife sounds. Glimpsing over to his dad, Sebastian noticed his concerned frown, which he tried to hide with a quick, unconvincing smile. Even Silas held close to his pant leg, his ears perked up and his tail hanging low.

Reaching the crest of a hill, Sebastian and his dad saw silhouetted traces of the border crossing through the fog. With no lights showing from inside, he guessed that the Canadian border agents were no longer guarding this point of entry into the country. The faint outline of a barrier spanning the width of the road also suggested this. Passing a sign on their right showing the name, *Seneca Gorge*, Sebastian nervously asked, "Dad, will we be able to cross here?"

"I hope so, kiddo. Otherwise it will be a long walk to New Hampshire before we can find another place to enter Canada."

Approaching the border station, the fog dissipated enough in revealing a chain-link fence and concrete barriers positioned across the entrance leading onto a long bridge. "Do you think it's an electric fence?" he asked when they stopped walking in front of it.

"There's one way to find out," his dad answered as he picked up a rock. Tossing it against the fence, the rock ricocheted to the left, causing no sparks. "I think we can climb it." Slowly reaching his hand out, his fingertips traced over the chain links without injuring him.

"What about Silas?"

Pointing over to the right, Lee answered, "He should be able to pass through that hole at the bottom of the fence. Do you think you're strong enough to make it over this?"

"I'll try," he quietly answered, unsure if he'd convinced his dad, or even himself, if he could. He watched his dad toss their backpacks over the fence.

"You go first, kiddo, just up to the top and wait there for me."

Swallowing hard before releasing a deep exhale, Sebastian gripped the mist-dampened chain links, pulling himself slowly up the fence. Several times, the tremors in his hands nearly made him lose his hold, but he held on, soon to rest at the top. With ease, his dad joined him there a minute later.

"I'm going to climb down first so I can catch you if you fall. Are you okay?"

"Yeah," Sebastian mumbled, keeping his balance while feeling the fence noticeably sway.

A moment later his dad called from below, "Okay, kiddo, try to ease yourself down." Hauling his leg up over to the other side, Sebastian climbed down, exhaling with relief when he felt his feet touch the ground.

Stumbling a bit with his balance slightly off, he moved over to the low hole in the fence. "Come on, boy," he urged Silas. Resting on his belly, the dog easily scooted through the opening and then knocked Sebastian to the ground by playfully pouncing on him, wanting attention. "Good, boy," Sebastian rewarded Silas, stroking the fur on the sides of its head.

Reaching out, his dad pulled him to his feet before turning toward the bridge, which at first glance appeared clear for walking across even with the thick covering of fog clinging to it. Spying over the edge, billowing mist ascending from the gorge depths reminded Sebastian of steam rising from boiling water. He could even hear the sounds of a flowing river hidden far below from view. Yet this first glance proved deceiving while cautiously stepping forward.

Silas's low growl alerted them of something blanketed by the fog. Anxiously looking to his dad, he saw how he'd covered his mouth and nose with his hands. "Cover your mouth and nose, kiddo. It reeks really bad here. It's burning my nostrils."

"I can't smell anything."

"I know, but I don't want you breathing too much of this in."

Looking down at his shoes, Sebastian noticed how the concrete had discolored, from light grey to a deep, dark charcoal shade. He then turned around, hearing Silas's whimpering while watching the dog prance and pace without moving forward. "It's okay, boy. Come on," he urged. Silas, however, resisted his command, remaining where he stood.

With another step taken forward, the reason for the dog's distress came into view. Kicking something hard, Sebastian glanced down and then staggered back when seeing the partially melted robotic torso and head of a replicate. Searching for his dad, he spotted his silhouette in the mist near the edge of the bridge. Maneuvering passed several other burned replicates strewn in his path, he soon was standing next to his dad, seeing what he'd found.

Littering the bridge before them was the scorched wreckage of a semi and its trailer. Through a large gaping hole, they discovered a multitude of melted replicates still emitting smoke from what must have been tremendous heat. "What do you think happened here?"

With his voice muffled while continuing to hold his hands over his face, his dad answered, "It looks like someone might have been trying to sneak these into Canada. The Canadian military must have discovered this. Judging from the damage to the trailer and the cab of the truck, and even the bridge, it took some pretty heavy firepower to stop it."

"Dad, where are the Canadian soldiers?"

"I don't know."

A sudden jolt under their feet was followed by cracks spreading out across the concrete. With his eyes bursting in their sockets, Lee uttered, "We need to get across the bridge, *now!*" Grabbing Sebastian by his backpack, his dad pulled him forward as a large piece of concrete near them broke free, plummeting into the fog-shrouded gorge below.

"*Silas*, come on, boy!" Sebastian yelled. The dog's barking echoed out but he still wasn't coming.

"*Come on.* We have to hurry!" his dad insisted, dragging him further away. Piece-after-piece of the bridge's surface quickly eroded behind them with each step taken.

"*Silas!*" Sebastian bellowed, completely panic-stricken. The dog's constant barking now competed with the crumbling sounds of the bridge's disintegration. "*Silas!*" he hoarsely called out when nearing the other side of the bridge. Lunging forward, both solidly landed on the road, each wincing with pain from the impact. Following a resounding thunderous crash, a thick rolling cloud of dust hid everything behind from view, covering them from head-to-toe with fine grey powder. And when looking out through the fading dust, they saw that the entire length of the bridge had fallen, including the semi and its replicate cargo.

Rising to his knees, Sebastian rasped out, "*Silas,*" only to be greeted with silence.

Reaching out for him, his dad coughed out, "*I'm sorry.*"

"*No!*" Sebastian angrily responded, bursting to tears. Pulling away from his dad, he lashed out, "No! I want my dog!" With his pulse racing and throbbing pain deep in his chest, the unleashing of the rage inside him spilled forth. "I want my dog. And—and I want to go home, only I don't have a home to go to. I'm cold and tired and hurt and want my hands to stop shaking. I don't want to have Parkinson's. I want all of this to be—*over!* Do you hear me? Do you?" Lee knelt in front of him, seemingly paralyzed by the torrent of his words. Breathless now, Sebastian whispered, "I wish—," without finishing his thought.

Now appearing angered, Lee growled, "You wish *what? Say it!* You know what I mean. So say it. Don't think I haven't. Don't think I haven't wished *every night* that you weren't here with me." Through his own streaming tears, Lee uttered, "I pray every night that when I wake up, you'll be gone, someplace far away where no one can hurt you. All those years ago, I couldn't protect you— and I still can't. Yes, I've wished that we never found each other, so I could continue to hope that you were alive and safe and away from all this madness." Exhaling deep, he finished, "So go ahead, and say it. Please. I've failed you too many times. I deserve to hear it."

Seeing the devastation so clearly masking his dad's face, Sebastian's heart sank even deeper, regretting his outburst. Within such a short amount of time his world had changed so violently, leaving his head spinning from all that had happened. In truth, he was homesick for the simple life that he'd made for himself before finding the *Daybreak* machine, eventually leading him to his dad. At the same time though, being with his dad meant everything to him, having never felt so safe, as crazy as it sounded considering now.

Sitting down on the ground and pulling his knees up to his chest, Sebastian mumbled with quivering words, "I— I—want—my dog." Burying his face against his jeans, his body shuddered while he cried.

Then feeling his dad's strong embrace from behind him, in his ear he heard his dad soothingly whisper, "I'm sorry."

Chapter Five

Attempting to flag down a car and a box truck, Lee wasn't really surprised that neither stopped, considering how filthy they both looked. Within an hour after the bridge collapsed, they came across a road and began walking west, in the direction he knew Montreal was. They'd maintained silence, barely sharing a glance at each other. And the heaviness of their footsteps seemed to drown out all other sounds.

Feeling guilty about what he'd said to his son, he wasn't sure where to break the invisible wall now separating them. But he knew his words, unleashed by fear and frustration, couldn't be taken back. Reminded on an old saying that you hurt the one you love, he knew he hadn't just hurt Sebastian, he'd destroyed him. Lee silently suffered his own punishment over this, believing he'd gone too far, beyond the point of forgiveness, both from his son and himself.

From time-to-time he would spy a glance at Sebastian, who looked back several times. Lee understood why, guessing that maybe he held hope Silas would be scampering to catch up to them. Yet each time he found him not following, Sebastian's forlorn expression mourned his dog's loss with growing sadness.

Stumbling to his knee, Sebastian unsteadily tried to stand. Stopping and reaching down, with noticeable hesitation, he took hold of Lee's hand, allowing him to help. And when starting out again, from the corner of his eye, Lee spied how much nearer his son walked next to him. Exhaling his fear, Lee eased closer until they were side-by-side. Sensing how this invisible wall might be evaporating, he attempted a breech, resting his hand on Sebastian's shoulder. Seeing how hard he swallowed, Lee felt emotionally overwhelmed when Sebastian mumbled, "When you wake up tomorrow, I'll still be here."

"So will I," he breathlessly whispered as the invisible wall vanished. Pulling his son to him, once again he said, "I'm sorry," and then continued, "I love you, kiddo."

Appearing in not wanting to make eye contact just yet, possibly suffering through his own shame, Sebastian uttered, "I love you too, Dad."

Startled by engine sounds behind them, both turned to see a semi, pulling a full log trailer, stopping on the side of the road. Leaning out the driver's side window, the driver called out with his noticeable French accent, "Need a ride?"

"Yes, sir. Much appreciated," Lee answered, with Sebastian following him back to the truck.

While climbing up in, the driver asked, "Where are you headed?"

"Montreal."

Scratching his thick beard, the driver said, "I can take you as far as Sherbrooke. There's a metro station near the truck stops that has trains running a couple times a day." Grinning, he added, "The truck stops have free hot showers. You'll probably want to freshen up and get some clean clothes. I don't think they'll let you on looking like this."

"A hot shower sounds great!" Lee commented with a smile.

Noticing how Sebastian was leaning to the side, seeming to have instantly fallen asleep, the driver mumbled, "The boy looks sick. Maybe I should take you both to the hospital instead."

Sighing, Lee revealed, "He's sick but his doctor, a specialist, is in Montreal. The doctors in Sherbrooke won't be able to help him."

"Then we'd better get moving," the driver said, pulling his truck back onto the road.

***

Stepping out of the truck stop shower, Lee watched Sebastian's trembling fingers struggling to tie his shoe laces. After pulling on jeans and a fresh t-shirt, he knelt down, double-knotting Sebastian's shoes for him. Then sitting next to him on the bench, Lee reached into his pocket, withdrawing a piece of paper which he handed to his son, along with half the money they had.

"What's this?"

"That address is where we're going after Montreal."

"Sea Bridge, Alaska?"

"It's a little town just outside Anchorage. I own an ocean-front home there. Actually *we* own it, plus a guest house on the property."

"What's it like?"

Grinning, Lee answered, "I don't know. I've never been there."

Smirking, Sebastian commented, "I keep forgetting how rich you are."

"You mean how rich I *used* to be. I bought that place, sight-unseen, with most of the untraceable cash I had left. I guess I'm going to have to work for a living once we get there."

"So why are you giving this to me?"

Easing closer to him, in a low voice Lee answered, "I don't want to scare you—but in case we get separated, I want you to go on to Alaska. You'll be safe there."

Studying the tremors coursing through his hands, Sebastian asked, "Is it because you think you'll fail again in keeping me safe?"

Swallowing hard, Lee answered, "I'm always afraid of that."

Understanding the fear gripping his dad, Sebastian leaned closer, wrapping his arm around his dad's neck. "I'm not," he whispered in his dad's ear, hoping to offer him some strength.

Seeming to force a grin on his face, his dad responded, "I love you, kiddo."

"I love you, too."

"Here, I want you to have this," his dad said, handing him an old pocket watch. "This used to be my grandfather's. It's always been my good luck charm. Now it's yours."

***

Blending in with several people entering the Sherbrooke metro station, Lee silently motioned for them to separate. Approaching a machine off to his left, he exchanged American dollars for Canadian and then went to the ticket counter, purchasing two passes for the next train to Montreal. Making certain not to directly face the numerous security cameras, he wandered over to a bank of vending machines, watching Sebastian's reflection through the dark glass on the first. He couldn't help but smile when noticing two teenage girls pointing at his son, clearly taken by his handsome features. Sebastian seemed oblivious as he reviewed the posted arrival and departure times.

Backing away from the soda machine, Lee halted when a security guard approached Sebastian. He tried to hide his concern of this as he wandered closer to them. "We don't allow runaways to loiter in the metro station," he overhead the guard say.

"I'm not a runaway. I'm traveling with my uncle to Toronto," Sebastian lied.

"Excuse me, officer," Lee interrupted. "Has my nephew done something wrong?"

Looking him over, the security guard responded, "No. We've had problems with runaways trying to spend the night here at the station."

Calmly, Lee responded, "I assure you, my nephew and I will be traveling on the next train to Toronto." Nodding his head, the guard walked away, turning back several feet away, still watching them.

"Do you think he believed us?" Sebastian mumbled.

"I don't know. I just hope this train comes soon. I don't like being so exposed."

"I know what you mean. Those girls behind us are bothering me."

Laughing, Lee asked, "What, not your type?"

Appearing to blush, Sebastian answered, "I kind-of liked one girl. Her name was Nikki. She kissed me, but I think it was because she was high."

Clearing his throat, Lee mumbled, "Maybe we should change the subject."

Seeing the lights of the approaching train, Lee and Sebastian walked down a flight of steps to a sub-level deck for boarding. Blending in again with the crowd of passengers, Lee noticed how they had fallen under the observing eyes of two more security guards. Holding his breath, he watched as one moved through the crowd and stood just off to his side. A chill ran down his spine when he heard the guard quietly say. "May I see your identification?" Relief flooded through him when he realized the question wasn't aimed at either of them.

Addressing a young blond-haired man standing to his left, the guard firmly gripped the young man's jacket, once more asking, "May I see your identification?" Speaking French and appearing to not understand the question, the young man turned around as if trying to ignore the guard.

"I'll need to see your identification, as well," the second security guard demanded, this time to Sebastian.

Fearfully looking to his dad, Lee interrupted, "What's the meaning of this? I already spoke to a security guard upstairs, telling him that my nephew and I are traveling to Toronto."

"Then you'll be disappointed in knowing that this train is going to Montreal, *not* Toronto," the guard responded.

"*Oh!*" Lee acted surprised. "I guess we're on the wrong platform."

"No, this is the right platform. However, the train leaving for Toronto doesn't depart until tomorrow morning." Smirking now, the guard insisted, "Both of you, come with me."

Before stepping out of line, the young man next to Lee threw a punch at the other security guard, stunning him. Looking frightened, the man bolted away, knocking several passengers down before being apprehended by the guard, with the one speaking to Lee rushing off to help. Struggling to free himself from the strength of their hold, both guards forced him down, pinning his face against the concrete.

With the train's doors opening, Lee quickly pushed Sebastian ahead of him onto the whitish-grey coach, finding comfortable seats near the door. Watching out their window, both saw the young man nearly break free but was again wrestled down. After the last passenger boarded, the closing of the coach doors was followed by a subtle lurch, as the train began its departure. Spying out the window for another look, both quickly fell backwards when the coach was jarred by the young man's head exploding, as if a bomb had been detonated. The impact of a robotic eye striking against the window held their final fleeting glances of the ensuing chaos.

***

Illuminated by glittering lights, the sprawling night skyline of Montreal glistened amidst the darkness outside the speeding train. "Look over there," Lee pointed out. "That's Olympic Stadium. Montreal is hosting next summer's Olympic games."

"Have you been here before?" Sebastian asked while trying to sound interested but in truth feeling too exhausted to care. He'd hoped to get some sleep on the train before arriving, yet after seeing the replicate explode back at the station in Sherbrooke, fear kept him restlessly on edge.

"I've been here a few times for business."

Leaning his head against his dad's shoulder, Sebastian asked, "Who are we going to see here?"

"A friend, someone I trust. Sidney used to work for Dryden in the pharmaceuticals division. He's brilliant. Ask him anything about medicines and treatments and he'll know the answer right away, kind of like you with solving complex math problems. He has a natural talent for medical knowledge."

"Why isn't he back in San Francisco, working in your offices there?"

"He left the company a while back for *personal* reasons."

Glancing down at his trembling hands, Sebastian yawned and then drowsily mumbled, "I hope your friend can help me stop shaking."

Resting his head next to his son's, Lee whispered, "I hope so, too, kiddo."

Chapter Six

Resting his head against the taxi's window, Sebastian saw the lighted buildings passing by, a mixture of historical and modern architecture. He watched the people casually strolling along, seeming untouched by the replicate global upheaval. He knew, though, how appearances could be deceiving, a lesson repeatedly learned.

"This place is so different from San Francisco," his dad quietly commented. "Montreal retains its charm of years past while embracing the future. It doesn't throw away things it no longer deems valuable, like San Francisco. Maybe that's why my friend chose to come here."

"Are we there yet?" Sebastian tiredly asked, causing his dad to laugh.

"After all we've been through, you're *finally* asking that," Lee commented, unable to stop smiling.

Turning down a side street, Sebastian felt the vibrations from the cobbled street the taxi drove over until it came to a stop before a row of vintage brick townhouses. Paying the fare, his dad motioned for him to get out, following him out to the sidewalk. "Come on, kiddo. This is the place."

Climbing a steep staircase, Lee knocked on the door and nervously exhaled. Movement from the other side could be heard until the silhouette of a person appeared on the front door's frosted pane. "Who is it?" a deep male voice called out from inside.

"An old friend," his dad replied.

Hearing several unlocking sounds, the door then opened a sliver with the man's face only partially in view.

"This can't be," the man responded, sounding confused. With the door flying open, a *woman* appeared in the doorway, a woman with rather *masculine* features. "*Get in here!*" she frantically urged. Passing quickly into the foyer, the woman then slammed his dad against the wall, holding a carving knife to his dad's throat. "What is my favorite song?" she rasped. "*Answer!*"

Swallowing hard, Lee blurted out, "Gloria Gaynor's, *I Will Survive!*"

Guardedly breaking her hold, the woman unexpectedly pulled Lee into her arms, vigorously kissing his cheeks.

"That is *probably* the first time in decades anyone could say that Disco saved their life," she said, her smile beaming. "I'm *so sorry* I put you through that. I had to make sure you weren't one of Lexia's deadly toys. Come on in," she urged. Stopping dead in her tracks, she turned to Sebastian. Looking oddly at first, her jaw dropped as she stared closer. Then covering her mouth while looking back and forth between him and his father, "No, it can't be." Reaching out, she softly touched Sebastian's face, tracing her fingers from one cheek to the next. "*Joshua?*"

"Sebastian," Lee corrected her.

Covering her face with her hands, she uttered, "*Of course*, Melinda's favorite name!" Dragging him to her, Sebastian's eye nearly burst from their sockets when his face was firmly pressed into her fake chest. "You look just like your father, and fortunately for you he's handsome, otherwise that would be a huge insult," she rambled on. Easing him away and allowing him to catch his breath, she continued, "I'm Sidney, one of your father's oldest and dearest friends. Come in, come in!"

As they followed Sidney down a long hallway, Sebastian whispered, "I thought you said your friend was a man?"

"He *used* to be," Lee answered.

"I still am, when the occasion calls for it," Sidney offered. "As a transgender, I still need to use to men's rooms in several states. You should've seen the stares I got when I entered a men's public restroom in Charlotte last summer."

Stepping into a large modern kitchen with white countertops and brushed-steel appliances, Sidney motioned for them to sit on bar stools at the large center island. "You boys look starved. What could I get for you? I was about to have some wine and cheese. And no, Lee, I don't have a drinking problem—*anymore*. I finally figured out that it's only a problem when you run out of alcohol."

Before Sebastian could sit down, everything in sight began spinning. Reaching for the back of the stool, his trembling hand missed with him falling to the floor. He heard his dad call out, "*Sebastian*!" as everything went dark.

***

"Boy, you sure do know how to make an entrance, don't you?" Sidney commented, checking Sebastian's pulse while sitting on the edge of the sofa. "You gave us both quite a scare."

"Dad," Sebastian mumbled.

"I'm right here, kiddo." Leaning over him, he saw his dad smiling.

"What happened?"

"You are one *sick* boy," he heard Sidney say. "Now I know why you came to see me."

"How long was I out?"

"About twenty minutes," Sidney answered, getting up to fetch his wine glass and a blanket.

Trying to sit up, his dad slid on the sofa, letting Sebastian rest his back against him. Draping his arm around him, his dad pulled him close as Sidney covered him with the blanket. "What do you think?" Lee asked, his concern clear in his voice.

Looking to them both, Sidney offered his diagnosis. "Well it's definitely Parkinson's disease, but *not* a natural strain of it. I'm thinking synthetic."

"*What*?" Lee burst out.

"The deterioration is advancing faster than it should, considering his age. With everything you've told me, I don't see how it could be any other way. Once I check the blood sample I took, I'm positive it'll confirm this."

Soothingly running his hand over Sebastian's chest, Lee responded, "So what you're saying is that this isn't natural. Someone *gave him* Parkinson's disease."

"Most likely by injection," Sidney guessed. "It could easily have happened years ago. The thing with synthetic disease strains is that they can be designed or manipulated to remain dormant for years until a catalyst of sorts occurs, releasing the strain. For Sebastian if may simply have been rising levels of testosterone in growing up."

"Would it have stopped this strain if he'd been inoculated against Parkinson's years ago?" Lee asked.

"I'm not sure," Sidney answered. "The strain inside him is more aggressive than I've ever seen before."

Listening to all this, a sense of hopelessness flowed through Sebastian. With tremors coursing through his body, he felt sick to his stomach and light-headed. What struck him most was the thought that someone had done this to him on purpose, showing extreme cruelty in wanting to harm him.

"Was it Lexia who did this to me?" Sebastian quietly asked.

Appearing startled by this question, Sidney held silent while his dad answered, "I don't know."

Seeming to compose himself, Sidney reached over, touching his cheek. "I'm going to do all I can to fix this."

"Where do we start?" Lee questioned.

Standing and pacing, Sidney cautiously glanced over, staring at Lee. "I have *one* idea."

"No," his dad firmly and quickly answered.

Pleading his case, Sidney continued, "Listen to me. In a diluted form, it could reverse many of the symptoms, if not all."

"No," his dad growled in response.

"Lee, listen to me. I've done extensive post-mortem research. I know where things went wrong. I've tested my results. I *know* this will work!"

"You listen to *me*," Lee insisted. "I *will not* under any circumstances, have my son injected with that poison."

Sidney angrily argued back, "But you're willing to let the other poison kill him!"

Sebastian begged, *"Stop it,"* covering his ears while tears streamed down his cheeks. Shuddering with fear, his chest heaved as he felt his pulse racing.

"I'm sorry; I'm sorry," Lee kept whispering, holding him even closer.

Covering his face with his hands, Sidney exhaled deeply while regaining control of his temper. Returning to the sofa, he sat of the edge, taking hold of Sebastian's quaking hand. "I'm sorry, too. We'll find another way. I promise." But there was something in his eyes that Sebastian noticed, an insincerity and strangeness that did nothing to lessen his panic.

***

Blankly staring out to the darkest corner of the bedroom, Sebastian listened to the night time sounds heard through the partially open window. A dog was barking somewhere close by and a car drove over the cobbled street. Pulling a quilt closer to him, he shivered a bit from a lightly chilled breeze disturbing the curtains.

His door unexpectedly opened, his dad stepping into the room. Wearing a pair of borrowed flowery pajama pants, he, himself, shivered while closing the window. Easing then into bed next to him, Sebastian heard his dad exhale and then faintly whispered, "I'll be here when you wake up in the morning."

"So will I," Sebastian whispered back.

"I'm sorry. I didn't mean to wake you, kiddo."

"I can't sleep."

"I understand."

Rolling over and staring up at the ceiling, Sebastian asked, "The stuff Sidney wanted to give me was the experimental drug given to Lydia and the others, isn't it?"

"Yeah," his dad softly responded. Leaning up, he added, "I won't let him do it. The risk is too great. There's got to be something else. We'll find it."

Exhaling lightly, Sebastian closed his eyes, desperately wanting to fall asleep but knowing that he couldn't.

***

After getting dressed, Sebastian headed downstairs. Rubbing his hand over a swollen spot on his neck, it hurt like a bee sting, although he couldn't remember having been stung. Hearing voices coming from the kitchen, he quietly approached but stayed just out of sight while listening to the conversation.

"Isn't it a little early to be drinking?" he heard his dad ask, sounding slightly annoyed.

"There's orange juice in it," Sidney offered in his defense.

"And vodka," his dad added.

"What can I say? Some work with hammers and wrenches, I work with screwdrivers."

"I pity your liver."

Following a moment of silence, speaking in a lower tone Sidney continued, "We need to talk about BE37."

"No. I told you last night, under no circumstances will my son be injected with that poison."

Arguing further, Sidney snapped, "Your son's condition is going to deteriorate further within a matter of weeks. BE37 in a diluted form can help him. Why won't you listen to reason?"

"Because it destroyed my daughter!" Lee angrily responded.

Softening his tone, Sidney uttered, "I regret what happened to Lydia but I know now how to fix it, and I *have*. If you will just look at the research with your own eyes. Lee, listen to me, I know how devastated you were when the full effects of the drug stole Lydia from you. And I know how it destroyed you when your son was taken away from you. You're my friend. I can't simply stand back and watch him being taken away from you again, not when I can do something to stop it."

"Damn, you," his dad mumbled. Deeply sighing, he then quietly said, "Fine, show me your research."

"It's right over here in my office. Go on in."

Sebastian was about to join them but stopped, startled by a door slamming shut. He then staggered back when he heard pounding and his dad yell, "Sidney, let me out of here! Damn you, let me out!"

"I'm sorry, Lee. I can't do that. Not until you face the truth. You know all about the truth, don't you? Plan on staying in there until nightfall."

Chapter Seven

Through grinding teeth, Lee growled, *"Sidney, unlock the door."* Pounding on the solid wood surface and twisting the doorknob proved futile. Hearing nothing from the other side, he bellowed out, *"Sebastian! If you can hear me, run!"* Resting his forehead against the door, he closed his watery eyes, trying to hold his emotions in. Robbed of his breath, his pulse raced as he attempted to regain control. "Please, Sebastian, run away," he whispered.

Rushing to the windows he searched for locks on both but found none. Grabbing a brass table lamp, he threw it against the first pane, only for it to bounce off the shatterproof glass. Pressing his face to the window, he frustratingly exhaled, clouding the window with his warm breath.

Turning around, his jaw dropped when finally realizing what this room truly resembled. Decorated with bright colors, a large part of the floor space was occupied by a child's oversized playhouse. Set on opposite walls were shelves displaying toys and books with a huge mural of nursery rhyme characters covering the wall surface across from the windows. The only thing not seemingly meant for a child was the modern-style desk positioned between the two windows.

Stepping back, his eyes were drawn to the screen of a laptop computer on the desk. Leaning down, he began reading the displayed information. Then sitting in the chair, he scrolled through several screens which summarized the brain enhancement drug's previous experiments, confirming successes and failures. Picture after picture of the human subjects appeared onscreen with

Lydia's image being the last. His heart broke as he studied her joyful expression, just how he remembered his daughter before the drug altered her forever.

Continuing his skimming of the information, Lee came across video footage of Lydia and Sidney. Thoroughly confused by their being together, he was just about to click the onscreen arrow for the video to play, but stopped when the door to the playhouse opened. His lungs held his breath hostage when he heard a cheerful greeting. "Hello Daddy!"

***

Hearing his dad call out for him to run, Sebastian rushed back up the steps to the bedroom, closing and locking the door behind him. Grabbing his backpack he tripped on the carpet, stumbling to the floor. Catching his breath while waiting for his lightheadedness to clear, he heard someone quickly climbing the steps and then noticed a shadow through the slit under the door. The doorknob turned twice but remained locked.

"Sebastian, please open the door," Sidney calmly asked from the other side. "I need to explain all this to you. I need for you to understand. Please don't be scared. Everything will be all right, I promise."

Slowly stepping over to the door, as Sebastian was reaching over to unlock it, he noticed a syringe with his name on the label that had been tossed in the waste basket. He reached up, running his fingers over the swelling on his neck. Remembering what they'd said about injecting him, Sebastian staggered back in fear. Knowing how his dad refused to allow the drug to be given to him, he suspected Sidney had injected him anyway during the night.

Backing further away and easing open the bedroom window, Sebastian glanced down, believing the drop to the sidewalk was only slightly lower than the chain-link fences he used to scale in San Francisco. Tossing his backpack out the window he scooted onto the window ledge and jumped, as Sidney began knocking on the door.

Pain shot from his ankle, forcing him to his knees. Grimacing Sebastian fought for his breath as his whole body quaked. But the adrenalin flowing through him allowed him to stand. Grabbing his backpack he hobbled away, hoping to disappear from sight as soon as he could.

Seeing signs for a nearby metro station, Sebastian headed in that direction but was halted when a police officer approached him. "Son, what happened to you?"

Anxious in wanting to get away from him, Sebastian lied, "Some guy, down the street, tried to steal my backpack. He kicked me in the ankle."

"Can I look at it?" The office asked.

"I just want to go home!" Sebastian blurted, barely keeping control of his nerves.

"If your ankle's broken, you need to get to a hospital. Let me take a look at it." The officer knelt down but Sebastian backed away.

"*Please*, just let me go home," Sebastian begged, tears welling in his eyes.

"It's okay, son. I know you're scared." Standing up, the officer asked, "Where's home?"

Swallowing hard, Sebastian uttered, "I need to take the metro over there."

"I should take you to the hospital and file a report of this."

"Please, I just want to go home."

Sighing and running his hand down his jaw, the officer said, "Okay, drape your arm around me. I'll help you over to the station. But when you get home, you have your parents look at that ankle."

"Yes, officer."

Aided by him, Sebastian made it across the street and down a flight of stairs to the ticket counter. While studying a map of the metro stops, the officer asked, "Where do you live, son?"

Wanting to get rid of him, Sebastian glanced over his shoulder and faked panic. *"The guy that jumped me just went in the men's room!"*

Signaling his dispatcher on his radio, the officer spun around to Sebastian. "Stay here, son. I'll need you to identify the suspect."

As he cautiously moved toward the men's room, Sebastian turned to the metro clerk. "I need a pass to the stockyards on the edge of the city." Moments later he hobbled away, boarding the metro and staying hidden until it pulled away from the station.

***

Upon his arrival at the West Stanley Metro station, Sebastian discovered an internet café next door. Wandering inside, he approached the counter and ordered hot chocolate and a pastry from the clerk. After paying, he found an empty seat toward the back. Taking a sip of his hot chocolate, he watched one of the patrons enter a numeric password on one of the keyboards. Brilliant with numbers he instantly remembered it. Then, rising from his seat, he found an available computer to use. Typing in the *borrowed* password, he immediately gained access to the internet.

He read several of the day's headlines as he ate his pastry. A deadly passenger train derailment near Toronto, a cyclone heading toward India and such. He thought for a moment over what he wanted to see. Sebastian typed in the name, *Lee Dryden*. Appearing on screen was his father's obituary, a clear fabrication mostly likely provided by Lexia. He noticed that neither himself nor his mother were mentioned, which didn't surprise him. However, what *was* mentioned made him angry. Lexia's vicious lies portrayed his dad as a criminally insane recluse whose self-righteous beliefs destroyed America by exposing government programs designed to keep the public safe. She cited the replicate initiative as being his brainchild, forcing as much blame as possible on his dad.

Too disgusted to read further, Sebastian pulled up a profile of Lexia. It showed her exoneration from all criminal charges, and that her husband was the true mastermind behind deceiving the American citizens. Now the chief executive officer for Dryden Technologies, her mission is to restore faith in the corporate giant she now helms and finding a way to stop the *Nightfall* program from releasing damaging information to the public.

Growing nauseated by how the article enhanced her reputation, Sebastian then typed in the name, *Lydia Dryden*. Lydia's obituary appeared onscreen. As a social media entrepreneur, he read how adored she was by an endless list of celebrities. Numerous tweets listed expressed how much the world adored her with pictures from a star-studded Hollywood gala honoring her as proof.

Uninterested by how Lydia was glorified in the media, he pulled up images on Sea Bridge, Alaska. Feeling more at ease in viewing the online pictures of the small seaside town, he wondered what life would be like there while hoping he could share this with his dad.

Sebastian's breathing grew rapid due to his guilt at leaving his dad at Sidney's house. Many times since running away, the thought occurred to go back for him. But in the end, he chose to do what his dad wanted him to do. But he missed him, and felt like a failure for abandoning his dad.

As he reached to turn off the computer, another thought occurred to Sebastian. He typed in an email address and then composed a message.

***

"Dad's gonna kill you, if you're on social media," Nikki commented while sitting down next to Scotty with her bowl of popcorn.

Without looking up from his computer screen, Scotty mumbled, "*Okay*, what do you want to keep quiet?"

Thinking a moment before smirking, she answered, "I get your turn with the jeep on Saturday night."

"Got a date?"

"None of your business," she snapped.

"What's his name?" he absently asked while typing on his keyboard.

Huffing and crossing her arms over her chest, Nikki reluctantly mumbled, "Clay."

"He's cute, dumb as a rock—but cute," he commented.

As Scotty was about to sign-off the internet, the icon for incoming emails appeared onscreen. Having received no emails since leaving San Francisco, he held his breath as he slowly reached over, clicking to access his account. A smile burst across his face as he read the incoming message.

Scotty,

I hope you and your family are safe. I miss you, my friend. I don't have much time and I won't be able to respond to you if you write back, but I'll send you a message again when I can. Take care. Oh, and ask Nikki if she still has a thing for soft grey eyes and remind her I have two.

S.

Now beaming, Scotty handed Nikki his laptop, saying, "I still get the jeep on Saturday night," while watching her smile and blush as she read the message. But he noticed something else, her guilty glance as she looked away. Probably embarrassment, he guessed.

***

After stepping outside the internet café, Sebastian decided to go back inside to use the restroom. Walking up to the clear glass door, he halted with his heart nearly bursting through his chest. Leaning over the laptop he'd just used was a man dressed in black, appearing similar to the man Dryden sent to the Lesterman farm. Now worried that he'd exposed Scotty and his family by carelessly sending his email, he knew he had to do something to protect them.

Entering the café, he made certain that the man saw him heading for the restroom. As he was closing the door, Sebastian could see the man slowly approaching. Pushing open a high window, he saw a large brown dog chained to a fence. Whistling to it, the dog began barking while Sebastian pulled his head back inside. Then sneaking into one of the two stalls he left the door slightly open. He balanced himself on the toilet seat, making it appear that he wasn't inside. Holding his breath, he heard the man enter and then listened to him talking, most likely on a cellphone. "The kid slipped out the bathroom window. I'm coming out the front. See if you can cut him off at the end of the alley."

Hearing him leave, Sebastian snuck over to the restroom door, peeking out. Seeing no one in sight, he quietly walked down the hallway and returned to the laptop. Noticing that the man's password attempt had been denied, he exhaled with relief, hoping that he'd failed in tracing his email to Scotty. Grabbing it, he casually walked out of the busy café, with no one apparently noticing he'd stolen it. Looking in both directions he breathed a sigh of relief when he saw that the man was nowhere in sight. Pulling his hood over his head, he wandered away, dropping the laptop in the first dumpster he came across.

Chapter Eight

Slowly passing the grave markers of several entertainment icons, a silver Rolls Royce came to a stop near a white marble mausoleum deep within the grounds of the Hollywood Forever Cemetery. Lexia climbed out from the backseat with the assistance of her driver. "Wait here," she instructed him before slowly walking over to the rod-iron gate sealing her daughter's grave. Littered about were sympathy cards, posters, balloon, small stuffed animals, and trinkets of all kinds, left by Lydia's adoring admirers. Smirking while kicking a few aside, Lexia typed a code number into a keypad, unlocking the door so she could step inside.

Running her fingers across the smooth surface of the crypt, this moment of paying her respects to her departed daughter was disrupted by the buzzing of her cell phone. Glancing at the number appearing on the screen, she then addressed her caller. "I expected to hear from you weeks ago."

"There were complications smuggling your *package* into the country," a deep male voice responded.

"And has everything been taken care of?" Lexia cautiously inquired.

"You mean, is this a *dead* issue?"

"There is no need to be sarcastic."

After a moment's pause, the male voice asked, "With all that you've done, I never imagined that you, of all people, would lose the nerve to handle something as simple as this."

Swallowing hard, Lexia responded, "I had my reasons for having someone else carry out this task."

"You're still being watched, aren't you? Even after being cleared of all charges, you're still under suspicion."

"And will remain so until I can stop *Nightfall*," she confirmed. "Now, you still haven't answered my question."

"You entrusted me with this task. Do you doubt my ability to see it through?"

"No."

"Yes you do—and with good reason," the man taunted her. "You see my dear, Lexia, after so many years of being apart, I found an *unparalleled* level of clarity—leading to discoveries that have changed my entire outlook."

"What do you mean?" Lexia asked, her hand growing red by the strength of her grip on her phone.

"I know everything. All your twisted lies have been exposed. Dear God, what a fool I was."

"What lies?"

"Where are you?" the man asked, deflecting her question.

"I'm at the cemetery in Los Angeles, paying my respects."

"Another brilliant performance, I'm sure. Lies must be well tended to." Sighing, the man responded, "You should fly up here when you have a chance. It's beautiful this time of year."

"You know I never travel that far north," Lexia anxiously offered.

"Maybe this will change your mind."

Her body shuddered with fear when she heard a familiar girl's voice. "Hello, mother."

****

Gripped by the paranoia of feeling watched, Sebastian attempted to stay clear of crowds and large open spaces as he made his way on foot to the train shipping yards at the edge of the city. Knowing he didn't have enough money to purchase a passenger ticket to Alaska, he decided his best option would be to hide in a boxcar on a train heading west. He had traveled this way before, from Lincoln, Nebraska to Youngstown, Ohio when heading across country, eventually finding his way to his dad's lighthouse in Maine.

Approaching the chain-link fence surrounding the shipping yards, for a moment he stood there, entranced by the sight of the bright orange-colored western sky, corrupted with the faint wisps of clouds. Reaching forward, his fingers entwined with the links as he continued staring at the last remnants of the sunset, surprised in being able to smell the industrial diesel scent from the nearby locomotives. Distracted by the distant barking of a dog and the sounds of cars speeding on a nearby highway, Sebastian momentarily forgot his reason for being here.

"Hey, kid, what are you doin' over there?" he heard a man call out from behind him.

Thinking fast, Sebastian faked his friendliest smile while turning around. "I was just watching the trains. They're a lot bigger than I remember them being. My dad used to bring me here to watch them before he died," he finished with his expression growing sad. Remembering something from earlier he continued his lie while looking away, "He was on the train that derailed near Toronto."

Appearing to struggle in finding something to say, the man could only manage uttering, "Oh. I'm sorry."

"Is it okay if I watch them for a few minutes?" Sebastian asked, almost pleading.

"Sure, kid," the man responded, sort of smiling at him.

"Where are they going?"

Hesitant with his approach, the man pointed through the fence. "The one to the left is going to Hamilton, tomorrow morning. That one over there, in the center, just came in from Calgary. And the farthest one, over there, is leaving for Vancouver in about an hour." Sebastian offered a smile to the man for answering his question. The man returned the smile, then added, "You best be getting home soon. It's not safe around here after dark."

Nodding his head, Sebastian replied, "Yes, sir, I will. In a few minutes, if that's all right? Mom's been crying a lot, and I'm just not ready to go home to that." The man nodded his understanding while seeming to fail in finding anything else to say.

Once certain he was alone after watching the man walk away, Sebastian slipped through a chain-link gap in the fence, just barely squeezing through. With his ankle still throbbing, he hobbled through some high grass, stumbling over a hidden railroad tie. Dropping to his knee, Sebastian gripped his injured ankle, now radiating with even more pain. Feeling nauseous and light-headed, he closed his eyes for a moment until both sensations passed.

When standing up, he saw lights moving in the distance. Knowing they were the beams from flashlights held by shipping yard security, he tried moving faster until reaching one of the last boxcars coupled to the train heading to Vancouver. Ducking underneath, he quietly emerged on the other side and began searching for a door that would slide open. When moving from one boxcar to the next he stopped, feeling for a moment that he was being watched. Turning around, he saw the strange-looking silhouette of a tall, thin man wearing a hat, lingering near a security light. Blinking, the man then disappeared from sight, leading Sebastian to believe his eyes were playing tricks on him.

Before moving on, he tilted his head, trying to read the company name and emblem printed on the side of the boxcar. There was something familiar about both, but being mostly covered by spray-painted graffiti made recognizing both impossible.

As he approached another boxcar, he heard a man shout out, "Hey, you there. Stop!" Nervously exhaling with chills running through his trembling body, Sebastian shifted to the side, expecting to be blinded by the flashlight's beam. Yet there was no one behind him. The warning to halt must have been meant for someone else, with Sebastian now believing that the man he'd seen was in fact real.

Continuing on, he finally discovered a boxcar door that would slide open for him. Pushing it aside as soundlessly as he could, he tossed his backpack inside first before climbing in. Inhaling the strong fragrance of wood, possibly cedar, he found a space between two large crates labeled with the words, *Made in America.* Crouching down, Sebastian held still. When glancing out into the darkness, at first he couldn't see anything. Then trembling with fear, he watched the bright glow from a flashlight beam seep in through slits on the door, revealing a veil of dust clinging to the air as if something was on fire. Appearing like the alien light probes from science-fiction movies, the glow moved around with its search. A moment later all returned to blinding darkness when the light outside dimmed and then went out.

Lightly breathing a sigh of relief in not being caught, Sebastian leaned back, resting against another crate. For a moment he began feeling drowsy but was jarred awake when he heard the boxcar door being shaken. Holding his breath with his pulse racing and his heart beating fast, he peered out from behind the corner of the crate. No one was there. Yet before he could relax, he heard the sounds of footsteps overhead. This soon stopped with silence returning for only a moment.

Sebastian heard the high-pitch of the train's echoing whistle. Bracing himself from his previous experience with traveling this way, his body slammed back against the crate when the boxcar lunged forward. The shuddering sensation of the train moving along its rails started slow at first and grew with intensity. This, coupled with his Parkinson's tremors, shook his body as if gripped with convulsions. Closing his eyes, he deeply inhaled, which proved a mistake as he started sneezing from all the dust.

Crawling on his knees across the quaking floor, Sebastian managed his way over in finding the door. Roaming his hand up, he pushed with all his might until it opened a sliver. Gazing out to the rapidly passing landscape, his eyes were drawn at first to the sparse lights from houses near the tracks and fireflies signaling out to each other.

He wondered what the people inside their homes might be doing, possibly getting children ready for bed or watching a program on television. Maybe they were chatting on Facebook or checking their emails. Before time spent with his dad at the lighthouse, Sebastian had never experienced the ordinary, everyday rituals and routines that made up a normal person's day. Fixing his eyes on one lit window after the next, he tried to imagine what his life would have been like had things been different. And he also thought about what life would be like when reaching Alaska. Would his dad be there waiting for him? What if he wasn't? What then?

As the lights from houses became more widespread, Sebastian's sight was lured up to the brilliant array of stars decorating the night sky. One star in particular appeared to outshine all others, causing him to remember the phrase *by the light of the nearest star*. Resting his head against the vibrating wall, with his eyelids growing heavy, he fought to continue gazing at the passing view. What struck him most as he drifted off to sleep was that as dark as it seemed inside the boxcar, in contrast, the land the train sped through appeared strangely lustrous, set aglow by the light of the moon.

Part Two

Close to Midnight

Chapter Nine

Tugging the blanket closer, Sebastian quickly remembered not having a blanket with him. Opening his eyes, he held his breath and watched a strange-looking man sitting near him, tending to a small fire burning in what looked like an old hubcap. Over his thin frame, the bearded man wore brown camouflage pants, a green t-shirt with a hole on his chest, a red and yellow striped scarf and the top hat and coat which reminded him of a circus ringmaster. Using a spoon, he stirred what smelled like chicken broth being warmed in its can. Sebastian was surprised that he could recognize its aroma since mostly losing his sense of smell. Glancing over the man smiled and unexpectedly greeted him.

"Good morning."

With uncontrollable tremors coursing through him, Sebastian just stared, uncertain how to respond. The flames of both the fire and a lit lantern cast moving shadows through the dark interior of the boxcar, reminding him of the last night he'd spent camping with his dad in Maine.

"You're trembling like a leaf in a brisk wind, but you don't have a fever. The broth should be warm enough in a minute. That will make you feel better," the man said.

Swallowing hard, Sebastian uttered, "I'm not sick. I have Parkinson's disease. That's why I'm shaking." Raising his eyebrows, the man looked surprised to hear this.

"I bet you're scared too," the man guessed.

"Yeah."

"You don't have to be. I won't hurt you," he continued, offering another smile full of kindness. "I'm Harry," he introduced himself.

"Sebastian."

Beaming, Harry commented, "What an awesome name to have, unique."

Sitting up, Sebastian guardedly asked, "Were you watching me in the train yards back in Montreal?"

"Yeah. I wanted to make sure you got on the train. I lured the security away so you could."

"Thanks."

"So, are you running away from home?"

Thinking at first to lie, Sebastian decided instead to tell the truth. "I'm going to Alaska to be with my dad."

"Things at home with your mom not so good?"

Slightly glancing away, Sebastian answered, "She died when I was four. I don't really remember her except from what my dad told me. I was taken away from my dad and since then I was passed around from foster parents to boy's homes until I ran away."

"You seem like a nice boy. I'm sorry you had it so rough."

"I survived," Sebastian offered, looking back to Harry.

Using a rag to wrap around the can, Harry poured the broth into two tin mugs, handing one to Sebastian. "Be careful; it's hot," he warned.

Leaning back against the boxcar wall and taking a sip of the broth, Sebastian then asked, "When did you climb in here?"

"Close to midnight. I came in through a hatch in the top and found you asleep."

Realizing he was still under the blanket, Sebastian started pulling it off but Harry stopped him. "You keep it for now until the chill's gone inside here."

After sipping more broth, Sebastian asked, "Are you going all the way to Vancouver, too?"

Grinning, Harry thoughtfully responded, "I suppose so, and then I'll hop onto another train and see where that one goes."

"You do this all the time?"

"Yeah, trains, freight trains like this are my home. It's been years since I rode on one of those sleek fancy passenger trains. Yes, I've been on all kinds, from automobile transports to livestock to circus. I've been riding the rails for about six, maybe seven years." Smiling, he added, "I guess you could say I'm what they used to call a *hobo* or *tramp*."

"Don't you have a family?"

With his expression turning somewhat blank, Harry answered, "I used to."

"I'm sorry. I—,"

"It's okay, kid," Harry interrupted. "They're better off without me." Seeing his confusion, Harry continued, "After serving with the Canadian Special Ops Forces in stabilizing Iran during their civil war in 2026, when I came home. I was diagnosed with Post Traumatic Stress Disorder. To say the least, I wasn't the best person to be around. It's funny that after nine years I still hear shots being fired and the sounds of explosions. I guess it will never go away."

Unsure of how to respond, Sebastian finished sipping his broth, handing the mug back to Harry. Wanting to change the conversation, he wondered aloud, "Where do you think we are?"

Standing up, Harry walked over to the boxcar door and opened it enough to look outside. "Well, judging from the forest landscape and the position of the sun, I'm guessing we're somewhere in western Ontario."

"What do you think this train is carrying?"

Crookedly grinning, Harry answered, "Want to find out?"

Standing unsteadily, Sebastian followed Harry over to one of the larger crates. Using a machete he'd pulled out from a long pocket on his pant leg, Harry pried the lid off, dropping it to the side. With Sebastian holding the lantern over the crate, he dug with his hands through what looked like straw. Reaching as far down as he could, Harry then leaned back up, empty-handed from his search. "It's only straw, and not even real straw. It's made of some sort of plastic.

"Why would anyone be shipping fake straw?" Sebastian asked.

"They wouldn't," Harry answered. Exhaling, he continued, "If I were to guess, I'd say that something was sent to Montreal in this crate and now the empty crate is being returned to Vancouver. I bet if we checked we'd find them all empty."

"Do you think the other box cars are like this one?"

Shaking his head no, Harry revealed, "We're in the only boxcar like this coupled to this train. The outside is painted red. All the others boxcars are new, shiny and black." Running his hand from one cheek, down over his chin to the other cheek, Harry added, "I knew there was something different about this train when it arrived in Montreal." He smelled his hands, wrinkling his nose while seeming lost to his thoughts for a moment.

"How is it different?"

"It was unloaded and reloaded with armed guards surrounding it. Not police but private security. I've never seen anything like that before, not even when I was in the military."

"Could you see what they were loading?"

"No, I couldn't get close enough." Stroking his bearded chin, Harry said, "Next to the engine is a single passenger coach with no windows. I saw some men coming in and out of it." Smelling his hands again, he seemed to then recognize something. Appearing anxious, he whispered, "I think I know what the answer might be, and I hope I'm wrong. I need to get to that passenger coach."

"So how do we get there?"

"No, just me. I'm more experienced at this. I don't want to risk you getting hurt." Pointing his finger up to the top of the boxcar, Harry added, "Up and out."

***

Climbing onto a crate, Harry turned back, looking at Sebastian. "You don't need to do this," Sebastian urged. "It's too dangerous to walk on top of a moving train."

Shaking his head, Harry responded, "We need to find out what's in these other boxcars."

"Why not just wait until the train stops?"

"Because the train might not stop—or if it does, there will be too many people around."

"Come on. Let me go with you. I'll be all right."

Reaching out, running his hand over Sebastian's head, Harry told him, "No. You stay here. Your shaking makes you too unsteady to handle the force of the wind on top of the train. I'll be back as soon as I can."

Stopping him again, Sebastian asked, "What do you think this train is carrying?"

"I'll tell you when I get back."

Sighing with frustration, Sebastian uttered, "Just be careful."

Harry smiled. "Thanks."

"For what?"

"Well, it's just been a long time since someone worried about me." Sebastian nodded his head, seeming to understand.

Forcing his shoulder against the boxcar's rooftop hatch, it burst open, sending a shaft of light and air gusting down inside. Once outside, Harry could hardly stand due to the wind's velocity over the speeding train. Staggering a few steps, he dropped to his knees, finding it much easier to move crawling on his stomach.

To his left, the pine trees lining the tracks appeared as greenish blurs. Believing that this train was traveling much faster than any other he'd been on, he found it hard to breathe when looking ahead. Needing to move forward, every so often he pressed his face against the boxcar, inhaling the pungent stench of tar while gasping for air.

Subtle and not so subtle turns in the tracks kept Harry sliding about the roof. After what seemed forever, he passed over the gap from one boxcar to the next, resting and summoning his nerves to move on. With the black surface baking by the midday sun, Harry felt the palms of his hands and his fingertips being scorched. Having nothing to cover them with, he painfully grimaced, certain he would soon have blisters. Needing relief, Harry rolled onto his back, using his arm to shield his eyes from the blinding sunlight.

Pausing for a few minutes, Harry's eyes were drawn the shimmering water of a river flowing next to the tracks. Panting and his throat dry, the thought of a soothing drink of cold water crossed his mind, adding to his misery. Another thought occurred to him, to return to Sebastian and wait until later, when the sun was going down. But he knew the tar surface would remain smoldering-hot until close to midnight. And he understood the dangers of doing something like this after dark with diminished visibility.

Continuing on, attempting to find something to think of to take his mind off the heat and stench, he began whistling, concentrating on the melody. However, he stopped this when he saw blood dripping down on the tar and guessed it was from his dried, cracked lips.

Exhausted from crawling over a dozen boxcars, Harry breathed a sigh of relief when finally reaching the passenger coach. Carefully lowering himself down between the coach and the last boxcar, he stood before a solid-metal door with no window. Reaching forward, his hand grasped the doorknob, expecting it to be locked. However, it turned with ease.

Pushing the door in just a sliver, he saw what looked like a control room with numerous computer and video monitors, as well as a detailed map of Canada. Seeing no one close by, Harry slipped inside, looking around for traces of anyone. Believing he was alone, he sat at one of the computer stations and was about to begin reading the information shown onscreen when a man's voice quietly addressed him. "I was wondering how long it would take you to get here. Where's your friend?"

Chapter Ten

Anxiously pacing while waiting for Harry to come back, Sebastian staggered to the left with the shift of the train. As he pulled himself up to his knees, he found a wallet there on the floor. Moving over to the partially open door for some light, he unfolded the wallet, wanting to see who it belonged to. The first thing he saw was Harry's military identification card, with his picture on it much different from the man Sebastian met when he woke up. Clean-shaven with short dark hair, he appeared well-groomed in his special ops uniform. Reading further, the information on the card revealed that Harry was born in Edmonton, Canada. His home address and phone number were also listed.

The remaining contents in Harry's wallet included seven dollars and some odd change. There was one other picture, taken on a beach of him with a woman and three young boys who looked identical. Turning the picture over, Sebastian read, *"Bermuda, 2023, Harry, Elaine, Dane, Drew, and Dustin."* They looked happy, leading him to wonder how things could have changed so much for them. He'd heard and read stories of men returning from war, altered forever by what they experienced. He felt sad for Harry, regretting how much he'd lost.

Stuffing the wallet into his pocket with the intention of returning it to him, Sebastian was about to begin pacing again when he heard a thump on the boxcar roof. Stepping over next to the crate Harry had opened, Sebastian started to climb but then held still when the beam from a flashlight shone down through the hole. Knowing Harry didn't have a flashlight when he left, Sebastian backed slowly away, stopping when he heard words exchanged between two men, neither of which were Harry.

"This is the last one. He's gotta be in here," the first said.

"He better be, or the captain will toss us off the train," the other added.

Grabbing his backpack and carefully climbing as quietly as he could into the open crate, Sebastian pulled the top up over to conceal him. Hearing more loud thumps near him, he knew the men had entered into the boxcar through the top hatch. Keeping his breathing shallow, he spied out through a narrow crack in the crate, watching the men as best he could.

They quickly discovered the low burning fire, one of them stomping it out with his boot and then kicking the hubcap toward a dark corner. The other found the blanket and mugs. "Show yourself. We're not going to hurt you," he calmly called out. "Your friend sent us here to bring you back with us. Come on, don't be afraid."

"Be *very* afraid," the other joked.

"Shut up, you idiot!" the first man growled. Now brandishing what looked like Tasers, the first man firmly said, "I'm going to give you to the count of three to come out. I don't want to hurt you but I will if I need to."

"Let's just torch the crates. That'll draw him out."

"And set the rest of the train on fire. *Brilliant*, moron," the first man scolded.

Wandering over to the darker side of the boxcar, they both began kicking the crates, trying to lure him out. But before they could reach his crate, one of the men received a message on what sounded like the buzz of a cell phone. "Come on," the first man said. "We need to get back. The commander said the radar shows a storm coming."

"What about the kid?"

"If he's smart, he'll jump off the train the first chance he gets."

"And kill himself doing so," the second laughingly commented.

"Put your gloves back one. Remember, that's not just tar up there. That crap is engineered to act as solar panels. That guy was lucky he didn't burn his skin off."

With the sounds of them climbing the crates, Sebastian held still, hearing the first man call out, "We're not playing around, kid. We know you're in here. If you want to live, you'd better find a way off this train before we find you."

His pulse racing and shaking with fear, Sebastian pulled the crate lid back a sliver, waiting for any reaction from the men. When certain they were gone, he lifted the lid off, dropping it to the side before climbing out.

Over the train's droning sounds as they sped along the rails, Sebastian heard what he thought might be thunder. Unsteadily walking over to the boxcar's sliding door, he opened it enough to fully see outside. The dense forest they'd been passing though was gone, replaced with a wide-open rolling plain that stretched endlessly ahead. And though the sky appeared calmly blue overhead with a few white puffy clouds scattered here and there, the sky over the western horizon seemed ominously dark. As he continued watching, several bolts of lightning struck the ground in the distance.

Leaning his head against the boxcar wall, Sebastian's heart sank, believing something terrible had happened to Harry. He'd been so kind to him, a debt he knew he'd never be able to repay. Harry wasn't coming back, that was certain. Also certain the men *would* return, Sebastian understood the need to leave the boxcar and find another hiding place. Judging from the train's speed, jumping to his death wasn't an alternative.

Hesitating with climbing until the tremors running through his hands eased, Sebastian carefully began scaling the stacked crates. Once reaching the top one, he rested there for a while, feeling drained of energy. As he reached up to the hatch door, a loud rumble of thunder seemed to shake the boxcar with the crates under him vibrating to the point of teetering to one side. The hatch door didn't budge an inch while he pounded on it. Only by kicking at it was he able to open it, the door wrenched off by the strength of the screeching wind.

Thinking his body would be cold when climbing out, he was surprised by the stifling heat, not only radiating off the hot-to-the-touch boxcar roof, but in the air itself. Feeling as if crawling toward a blast furnace, after just a short distance his body was drenched with sweat and unzipping his hoodie helped little. Sliding on his stomach, his white t-shirt soon turned black over his chest and stomach, and with the wind's velocity bearing down on him even the slightest movement proved difficult.

Reaching forward to the edge of the boxcar, Sebastian cried out when scalding his fingers on a metal piece. Rolling over, he looked out at the passing plains, noticing how much closer the storm front seemed. Even more menacing, though, was the sight of a funnel cloud and forming twister. All appeared to his eyes as being in slow motion, but he knew it wasn't.

Shifting his body back over onto his stomach, he pulled himself to the edge, glancing down then at the gap between the boxcars. Seeing a windowless door, he decided to lower into the gap to balance between two boxcars, hoping the impossible that it might open for him. When wedged next to the door, Sebastian tried pulling on the handle, nearly losing his balance when startled that it opened inward with ease for him.

As he moved to enter the next boxcar, the resounding roar of the train grew ear-splittingly louder.

Yet it wasn't the sound of the train that had grown louder, but the twister and its twin crossing the landscape. A wake of dirt and dust shrouded the points where they met the ground, leaving scars on the land behind them.

Hurling himself into the boxcar, he found his sight useless, surrounded by pitch-blackness with the door slamming closed. He'd collided with something, sending him down to his knees with pain throbbing from his shoulder. Pulling himself up, he attempted to open the door which he now found stuck. Jerking it several times did nothing but rob him of what energy he had left. Too tired to search around for a light, Sebastian slouched against the door, hauling his knees up to his chest so his chin could rest on them.

One thing immediately noticeable was that the space he'd entered was soundproof, for no traces of the outside storm could be heard. Hearing the echo of his shoes on the smooth floor, he wondered how wide open the space might be in front of him. There seemed also to be coolness in the air, which smelled sterile like a room in a hospital. Breathing this in, coupled with the airs coolness, his severe fatigue and the overwhelming darkness, Sebastian's eyelids grew too heavy to stay open. After yawning twice, despite fighting to stay awake he quickly fell asleep.

***

Coming to, slightly opening his swollen eyes, Harry held in a cough while looking down to see blood and saliva drooling from his pulsating-sore lips. Growing coherent after the punishing beating he'd received from the train's security guards, he slightly shifted his gaze around, trying to stay quiet and not alert them that he'd awoken after passing out. Bound with handcuffs to a chair, he struggled to free himself, but it was pointless.

Video monitors showing every part of the train lined the wall in front of him. Searching from one to the next, he soon found the boxcar where he and Sebastian had spent the night. Staring closely at the image displayed, there was no sight of Sebastian anywhere. Glancing at the other screens, Harry still couldn't see him, although several screens were dark.

Turning his head to the left, he noticed the Canadian map mounted on the wall. Highlighted in yellow, a path leading from Montreal to Whitehorse had been plotted. Instantly realizing that they were not, in fact, traveling to Vancouver, he wondered why the train was heading for the Yukon and what were they delivering there. Thinking for a moment, the only place of real importance near the Yukon was—*Alaska*. That's it, the reason they're heading north.

When Alaska broke away from the United States during the anti-replicate uprisings, it crippled America by withholding much needed shipments of oil to force the recognition of their independence. With only Russia, China, and Mexico's support for Alaskan independence, America has been waging an economic war of attrition with their breakaway northern state, much like the policy they've continued using against the New England states and Texas. And while the Canadian government is sympathetic to Alaska's plight, the Prime Minister may have bowed to pressure from the American President in allowing use of its rail system for efforts in regaining control of Alaska.

Although realizing how potentially serious this was, Harry brushed it aside, wanting only for Sebastian to be safe and somehow escape if he could. Thinking of his own sons far away, he knew that a true father would do anything to save his children. Being with Sebastian helped him remember what it felt like to be a father. He didn't want to fail him—but knew he couldn't help.

Chapter Eleven

After dark, standing on the shore and spying through his binoculars, Abdul released a concerned sigh while watching distance ships signaling out to each other.

"What do you see?" Scotty quietly asked.

"The blockade military vessels contacting each other by Morse code. Their messages go undeciphered as most people aren't familiar with this obsolete form of communication."

"Can you tell what they're saying?"

Grinning, Abdul answered, "All's quiet."

Seeming hesitant, Scotty questioned, "Do you think there will be an invasion?"

Contemplating for a moment before answering, Abdul responded, "No. I believe all breakaway states, including Alaska, will return to the Union, *possibly* more as commonwealths than states, similar to how Puerto Rico is. I believe they will possess certain levels of autonomy. Lawmakers in Boston have begun deliberating over proposals from Washington regarding such changes. I expect Alaska and Texas will follow their lead. Any acts of aggression from Washington would damage these delicate negotiations."

Glancing over at Scotty, seeing how he nervously was shifting his weight from one foot to the next, prompted Abdul to change the subject. "Let's talk about you, and what you're not telling me."

"I'm not hiding anything," Scotty defended himself while failing to look at his dad.

"Spoken like a guilty man," Abdul commented, now perceptively staring at his son. "And *what* do I always say?"

Seeming to exhale his defeat, Scotty answered, "The truth shall set you free."

"And are you ready to rid yourself of the lie that holds you hostage?"

Sighing deeply, Scotty explained, "It's—not *really* a lie. I—got an email from Sebastian."

With his eyes enlarged with surprise, Abdul asked, "And what did it say?"

"He said that he hopes we're safe. He said he didn't have much time and couldn't write back if I responded." Scotty then blurted, "I know you said not to access my old email and social media sites. I—just—couldn't stop myself. I'm sorry."

Draping his arm around Scotty, Abdul smiled before saying, "Thank you for telling me this. Please, no more secrets. If he contacts you again, I want you to tell me right away."

"I will."

"Now, what do you take of his message?" Abdul continued.

"My gut feeling is that something's wrong."

"Mine too," Abdul agreed.

***

Groggily rubbing his eyes, Sebastian opened them to the same pitch-blackness from before. After stretching his tired body, he stood up, leaning back against the door while feeling light-headed and slightly off-balance.

Hoping that another door might be at the opposite end of this boxcar, Sebastian decided to risk walking through the dark to find it. Exhaling with his arms outstretched he began taking small steps forward. Anticipating obstacles in his path, though startled, he wasn't surprised when encountering the first. Adding to his growing fear, a faint humming sound then corrupted the silence, causing him to look around in trying to locate its source.

Reaching out, his fingertips touched something smooth and hard. Gliding them down the length of this, his fingers soon discovered a hand, the shock sending him staggering backwards. His quaking body once more pressed against the door. He noticed the soft flicker of light from both the roof and the floor. Flickers turned to flashes, illuminating the inside of the boxcar and revealing the train's unimaginable cargo.

***

From the corner of his eye, Harry noticed how one of the video monitors that had been off suddenly turned on. His jaw dropped and with his heart in his mouth, he saw all being revealed. Worse, there Sebastian stood, cowering against the fall, clearly frightened by what he'd found.

Hearing someone approaching, Harry knew he'd need to keep their focus away from the video monitors. Thinking fast, a plan formed in his head. When the security guard entered, he asked, "Did you bring me some lunch, or at least a beverage? As your guest, I would at the very least expect you to offer me some coffee and Danish?"

Smirking, the security guard answered, not with words, but by spitting on his face. "Well, I know where *your* mouth's been. The other guard is kind of cute," Harry commented, knowing his remark would be taken crudely and set the security guard off wrong. And he found success.

Leaning close to Harry, the security guard's face appeared red with anger. But before he could utter a word, Harry lunged forward, bashing his forehead against the guards, sending him unconsciously down to the floor. *"Damn, that hurt!"* Harry growled, wincing from the pain which left him seeing stars. As his blurred vision cleared, though the throbbing in his head continued, he watched

Sebastian on the video monitor, feeling worried and helpless to do anything.

***

Breathing heavy with his pulse racing, Sebastian's eyes fixed upon endless rows of replicates, both in front of him and suspended from above. But their numbers were merely an optical illusion, which he realized when glancing to his right, seeing his reflection. The walls inside the boxcar were paneled with mirrors, multiplying the true amount of replicates.

Struck by how everything in sight resembled the storage space of a high-tech factory, Sebastian took several steps forward, stopping before the first replicate. Clad in head-to-toe full body-armor and holding a high-caliber weapon, the replicate soldier appeared lifeless while standing there. Easing the visor of its helmet up, Sebastian saw its blank expression. Realizing the replicates required programming to become lethal and noticing the lack of external links, he understood that a simple remote command would bring them all to life.

Staring at the replicate in front of him, he knew there was no way he alone could damage each one separately, enough to stop them. "So how do you destroy a train full of deadly replicates?" he quietly asked aloud. The obvious answer then came to him. "Destroy the train, destroy the replicates." Continuing his thought process, he remembered reading the newsfeed at the internet café in Montreal about the recent train derailment in Toronto. "So how do you derail a speeding train?" Sebastian knew the answer to this could only be found in the engine pulling the train.

Walking slowly past the other replicates, he soon came to realize that all held the same facial image, leaving him wondering who the model for these soldiers might have been. Whoever he was probably suffered the same fate as the Lesterman's son, Ben. What happened to him? Was he still alive? Does this soldier's family miss him?

This last question forced Sebastian to confront being without his dad, worrying about what Sidney would do to him. He, himself, now shared his dad's guilt of abandonment. Truly they were so much alike, unable to keep each other from harm. Hoping to someday see him again, Sebastian resolved that the first words he'd say to him would be "I'm sorry."

Continuing on, Sebastian confirmed that there was a door opposite the one he'd entered over on the other side of the boxcar. Taking a deep breath, he pulled this door open, feeling the rush of wind on his face. As he expected, in front of him on the next boxcar was a door waiting to be opened, to reveal the continuously familiar cargo.

***

From what he could tell, there were only two security guards manning this control room. With one unconscious at his feet, Harry's mind worked fast in trying to figure out how to get rid of him before the other security guard returned. Gluing his eyes to the video monitors, he saw one conductor driving the train on one screen and what appeared to be the commanding officer visibly reprimanding the other security guard. A question occurred to him. Why was such a dangerous cargo being guarded by so few? But he quickly knew the answer, more guards would have drawn unwanted attention to the train. And the fewer who knew about it, the better.

"Now how do I get rid of you?" he whispered to the security guard passed out at his feet. Harry knew of only one way. Bouncing in his seat, he scooted it across the floor, over to the door leading out. Resting his jaw on the handle, Harry ground his teeth as he forced it down. At first it only moved slightly. Breathing hard, he again tried to open it in the same manner as before, coming so close but still failing. Muttering obscenities under his breath, Harry tried a third time. While his body shook violently, with all his might he pressed his jaw down upon the door handle, this time finding success.

Flying open, the door battered against to the side with the screeching wind deafening him. Bouncing in his chair, he returned to its original point, stopping for a moment in fighting to catch his breath. After doing so, Harry relentlessly kicked at the unconscious security guard, moving his body closer and closer to the open door, made easy by the polished smoothness of the floor. Once there, after several vigorous thrusts with his aching legs he managed to kick the security guard out the door. His body plummeted to the couplings before falling down to the rails.

After the door unexpectedly slammed shut, Harry glanced up to the video monitors. Watching Sebastian move from one boxcar filled with replicates to the next, he felt helpless in knowing how dangerous this train was and fearful for Sebastian's safety. And then the video monitor went dark. Holding his breath in waiting for the next darkened video monitor to come on, Harry then started mumbling, "Come on. Turn on. You should be turning on. Why aren't you turning on? You son-of-a-bitch, turn on." But it stayed blank.

***

Entering the next boxcar, Sebastian realized how different this one seemed compared to the others. With step-after-step taken, no lights turned on to reveal what he thought would be more replicates. Expecting to collide with something there in the dark, he didn't react fearfully when he knocked something over, which loudly echoed out. Not wanting to know what it was, he maneuvered passed it until kicking something that rolled away from him.

When moving further through the darkness, he stumbled over some low boxes before running into some large crates. Managing to step passed them, he discovered a small gap between the stacked crates, leading to another door. Opening this one, he instantly saw the entrance to the passenger coach.

Hoping that Harry was still alive, Sebastian wondered how to get inside to help him. Simply knocking on the door wouldn't be wise if he wanted to continue living. But as he stood there, thinking of how get inside, an idea formed in his head to *include* knocking on the door. And while turning away to find that which he needed, the light flooding in through the door revealed a word printed on the crate he stood next to; *ammunition*.

Chapter Twelve

Entering the control room, the second security guard appeared confused by finding Harry alone. "Where the hell did he go?" he asked as he scanned the video monitors for the other guard.

"I believe he fell off the train," Harry remarked.

"*Quiet*, or I'll push *you* off," the guard responded.

A loud knock on the door leading to the boxcars startled them both. Harry held his breath, worried that somehow the other guard *hadn't* fallen, although he thought he did. His heart then nearly burst through his chest when the security guard adjusted a video monitor to show who was standing outside. All they could see was Sebastian's red hoodie. Turning on the intercom, the security guard spoke into it, "About time, kid."

"Please let me in," they heard Sebastian beg.

Turning off the intercom, the security guard smirked and mumbled, "I'll let you in, all right." Withdrawing his Taser from its holster, he held it out and gripped the door handle. Jerking the door in, he jabbed Sebastian in the face with the Taser and instantly received a jolting electric shock. A shower of sparks set Sebastian's hood on fire, with his body falling away, though *not* his body but a replicate's instead. As the smoke cleared, Sebastian, missing his hoodie, appeared unharmed in the doorway.

Staggering to the side, they both watched the security guard's body convulse. And taking one final breath, he stopped moving. "I killed him," Sebastian whispered, his eyes large.

Thinking fast, Harry lied, "It's a replicate, a pretty advanced one too."

"A *replicate*," Sebastian uttered, seeming bewildered. "Was the other one also a replicate?"

Certain he wasn't, Harry answered, "Yeah, but you don't have to worry about him. He fell off the train," he finished, seeing relief flood over Sebastian's worried expression. "Get his keys so you can unlock these handcuffs." After finding the keys, Sebastian freed Harry. Pulling him close for a hug, Harry kissed him. "Don't scare me like that again. My heart can't take that."

"I'm sorry," Sebastian replied, still confused.

"Don't be," Harry corrected him. "You were freakin' brilliant."

"What do we do with him?" Sebastian asked.

"It's about time you did some chores. Take out the trash," Harry grinningly answered.

"Yes, sir." Dragging the security guard by his feet, Sebastian forced him over to the door and then kicked him out, the guard's body thumping against the boxcar before disappearing. Picking up the Taser, he examined the charred remains and then tossed it aside.

Searching the video screens, Harry spied the commanding officer talking with the conductor. Having no weapons, he knew he'd have to lure him to the control room and then overpower him. But before he could tell Sebastian his plan, he watched as the conductor and commander began fighting for control of the train. Pinning the commander to the wall, the conductor pulled out a gun, pressing the barrel to the officer's head. As he pulled the trigger, the commander grasped the barrel, quickly aiming the gun away from him. The bullet struck an electrical panel, resulting in a jarring explosion which sent tremors through the passenger car as the video monitor went blank. "*Damn*," Harry muttered.

"What?" Sebastian asked, easing up to Harry's side.

"I'm not going to lie to you. Things just got real bad for us. Come on."

Both passing through a bunkroom, having a small bathroom and kitchenette, Harry smelled smoke when they reached the control room door. Trying the handle, the door opened just enough to allow billowing smoke to seep out. Forcing it further in with all his might, Harry squeezed through the opening, finding the commander dead, his body smoldering from severe burns he'd suffered. Robbed of his breath by the wind's velocity penetrating through a gaping hole in the window, Harry noticed blood dripping from the jagged edges of glass. The conductor's body was missing, leading Harry to believe he'd been blown out by the force of the blast.

Surveying the damaged control panel, its charred surface appeared powerless, yet the train continued barreling along the tracks. Assuming the conductor never really had control of the train, Harry now guessed that the train was being remotely controlled.

A flash of light far ahead drew Harry's eyes down the rails. "Oh *Jesus!* When it rains, it pours." Well in the distance, but coming closer, a telltale-glow and pillars of smoke foretold the unthinkable. Swallowing hard, he prepared himself to tell Sebastian that things were about to get too hot.

Squeezing back out and closing the door behind him, Harry turned to Sebastian. "Follow me." Both stepping back into the control room, Harry spotted the map of Canada, seeing a blinking light which he knew to be their position, heading into Alberta. Tracing his finger along the mapped rail lines, he sighed, finding no intersections close to them. There was a branch of track however, shown near Canmore, that could prove useful should they survive the wildfires they were heading into.

"I don't get it. Those security guards acted more human than I'd ever seen replicates act before," Sebastian commented. "I could always tell in the past. There was something fake in how they spoke."

Without looking at him, Harry lied again, "I've heard rumors about a new generation of replicates, ones so advanced that you can't even tell anymore."

"How do you fight something like that?"

"I'm not sure you can." Turning away from the map, Harry asked, "Any experience with computers? My wife worked as a computer programmer, but I was never very good with them."

Shrugging his shoulders, Sebastian answered, "Enough to get by." Seeming lost in thought, a smile crept across his face as he added, "But I know someone who could help." Pulling a chair up, Sebastian placed his fingers on a computer keyboard, but couldn't control the tremors in his hands to begin typing.

Resting one hand on Sebastian's neck with the other covering the hand on the keyboard, Harry grinned and offered, "Just tell me what to type."

***

Peering over the laptop computer in front of him, Scotty saw the school librarian busy helping another student. Minimizing the screen his homework appeared on, he then accessed his private email account, knowing full well he'd earn a week's detention if caught. Surprised to receive an unexpected message, a rush of air loudly escaped his lungs, prompting a nearby classmate to hush him. Silently reading, *I need your help-S,* Scotty knew right away the source and importance of this. Clicking on the email, when coming up on screen, he read the following.

Scotty,

No time to explain. I need you to access the Canadian Railway database and search for any trains entering the province of Alberta, one heading toward Calgary. The conductor is no longer in control of the train.

I need you to stop it, if you can. If you can't, then I need you to divert it to tracks running south of Canmore, Alberta. Hurry, please. S.

Knowing any response might be picked up, either by the school or an unwanted third party that might be monitoring Sebastian's email, Scotty deleted this message, hoping there wasn't enough time in tracing it to him. Closing out of his private email, Scotty then pulled up the official website of the Canadian National Railway System, just as the librarian was approaching.

Mister Dominic, whose sour disposition matched the expression on his face, looked over Scotty's shoulder, glancing at the laptop's screen. "What are you doing?"

"Research for a project on North American Railroads," Scotty lied without looking at him. "You have no idea how *fascinating* this truly is," he said.

"Of course, I do," Mister Dominic remarked. "For nearly twenty years I worked for West America Railroad."

"*No kidding!*" Scotty acted impressed.

"Best job I had, before babysitting you brats here at the school."

Quickly devising a plan to use Mister Dominic as an unwitting accomplice, Scotty asked, "I have a question you might be able to answer. Say you have a train traveling at high speed where the conductor is no longer in control. Could the train be stopped remotely?"

Sitting down next to Scotty, Mister Dominic seemed lost in thought and then responded, "With all the modern technology running these trains, it's possible—but highly unlikely. You would have to know who was controlling the train. In this day and age, that source could be from either a central dispatch center or a satellite link. It could take hours to figure it out."

"Then how would you stop it? Say there were passengers in danger. How could you save them?"

Appearing thoughtful, Mister Dominic answered, "First, I would divert it to a track not in use by another train. I'd then cut all external power to the rails, figuring of course the train is like most modern metros, drawing power from the rails rather than the engine. That should do the trick."

"Thank you, Mister Dominic. You've been very helpful."

Crookedly smiling, Mister Dominic whispered, "Just don't tell anyone. I have a nasty reputation to uphold."

"You're secret's safe with me."

Once the librarian wandered away, Scotty began his computer wizardry in hacking into the Canadian Railway database. But from that point on, nothing proved easy as he soon discovered he wasn't the only hacker in their system. Tempering his frustrations, he found each move through the program to be countered and blocked by the other hacker, one far more sophisticated in the art of code breaking and data breach.

Understanding how overmatched he was, Scotty chose a simpler path, bypassing the main database and instead conducting a primitive search for crumbs, the remnants of past deletions. Programmers, as well as hackers, leave these traces. Keeping the other hacker blind to his new approach by issuing rapid random-access requests that eventually led to a systems overload, Scotty soon found the backdoor he desperately needed, slipping through unnoticed.

***

"Do you trust this friend of yours?" Harry asked while glancing at the video monitors.

"I'd trust him with my life," Sebastian quickly answered.

"What if he doesn't read your email?"

"He will. From morning 'til night he's online, even when it doesn't look like he is."

Before Harry could say anything else, he noticed that the lights in each of the boxcars carrying the replicates had suddenly all come on in unison. "What—do we—have—here?" he mumbled. Glancing closer to one of the screens, one of the replicates turned his head toward the video camera and pointed his weapon. Within the blink of an eye the monitor went dead, as did all the others.

***

Accessing the data Sebastian requested, Scotty discovered three trains entering Alberta, two heading for Edmonton and one heading toward Calgary. By the considerable speed listed for this last train and its position being the closest to Canmore, he knew this was the train Sebastian needed stopped, and guessed he might be on it. And with this information, Scotty saw a warning. The train's path would be crossing through a raging wildfire, scorching the forest terrain in that part of the province. All attempts to contact and halt the train had failed.

Adjusting his search to the tracks near Canmore, Scotty found easy access to all control programs for this part of the railway. Feverishly typing on his keyboard, he found success in diverting the rails, which would send the train south. But in doing so, too late he realized that the tracks lead to a dead end in an isolated area between the Canadian and American borders. Attempting to alter his command to divert, Scotty was kicked out of the database by the other hacker whom had found him. Each further attempt to regain access was frustratingly met with failure. "What have I done?" he whispered to himself while near tears, his stomach in knots and his pulse racing.

Chapter Thirteen

"We gotta get out of here," Harry warned. Walking over to the door, Sebastian watched as Harry cautiously reached out for the doorknob, almost seeming afraid to touch it. Releasing a deep breath, he opened the door, peering outside from behind it. "Come on. *Hurry!*"

Stepping over to follow him, Sebastian stopped when Harry leaned back in. Over the roar of the wind Harry called out, "There's a metal ladder on the right side of the boxcar. Follow me up it. We're going back to the boxcar we were first in. Cover your mouth and nose with something and stay low. Don't be scared. I won't let anything happen to you."

Tearing at the bottom of his white t-shirt, Sebastian ripped enough away, wrapping the fabric around his head, tying it to fit over his nose and mouth. After taking a few breaths, he moved over to the entrance. Heated air scorched his exposed arms and torso as he began climbing the ladder after Harry. Reaching the roof of the boxcar, Sebastian held still, gripped by fear.

Blistering heat made him feel light-headed as he watched the surrounding firestorm, mostly seeing a reddish-orange blur by the speed of the train. Everything in view had been engulfed by the wildfire. When able to focus, he saw raging flames consuming tall pine trees, making them look like towering torches. The fire bent and twisted around its wooden victims, reminding him of how snakes trapped prey in their coils, suffocating those that struggled.

Harry tapped on his shoulder, saying something he couldn't hear over the sounds of the deafening inferno carried by the bellowing wind. Motioning for him to follow, Sebastian could only manage a near crawl, searing his stomach on the boxcar's sweltering surface when touching it. His trembling hands suffered far worse, the skin red with pain.

Glancing to the sky, dark plumes of smoke shrouded the sun from view, making the sky seem as if it was just after dark. The sparks reminded him of fireflies he once chased on a warm summer night a long time ago. Larger pieces of burning brush thrust upwards by intense gusts appeared as Chinese lanterns, soon disappearing from sight.

Being dragged along by Harry, they soon reached the other side of the boxcar, standing as best they could before leaping over to the next. Stumbling and landing on his stomach, he burned his abs but continued following, although growing weaker with every movement. A flurry of hot ash was captured by the wind, falling over them.

After jumping to the next boxcar, Sebastian staggered onto Harry. Looking back, they were just to continue moving on when a vibration underneath halted them. Blinding flashes of fire consumed the air within the black boxcars when each one's doors automatically opened. From where they lay, Sebastian and Harry watched as some burning replicates dropped lifelessly out, falling near the tracks. Other replicates managed to climb up to the boxcar roof, only to disintegrate to ash. One, however, stood up and aimed its weapon at them. Violently shaking, the weapon discharged with the barrage of bullets passing over their heads. Immersed in flames, the replicate dropped to its knees.

Everything in sight began spinning with Sebastian no longer able to focus. Trembling uncontrollably, each breath he fought for grew shallow. Harry's worried face came into view but Sebastian couldn't keep his eyes open.

***

"*N*o!" Harry yelled, pulling Sebastian closer to him. Gasping for his own breaths, Harry felt himself giving up, bursting to tears while tenderly running his hand over Sebastian's cheek. Then taking a deep breath, his attempt to try standing was stopped when the train veered left off the main rails, nearly knocking them both off the boxcar roof.

The smoky stench of the fire held thick in the veiled air, but what remained of the forest continued burning with far less flames. Glancing about, Harry saw the charred ruins of a once dense forest for a far as his eyes could see. Not one tree or bush had been sparred its wrath. Before looking away, a shaft of sunlight pierced through the thick, overhead blanket of smoke, as if absolution had been pronounced over the devastated landscape.

Looking down he thought for sure that Sebastian lay dead in his arms, until the boy slightly moved his head. With his heart pounding, Harry did everything he could think of to revive Sebastian, even sharing his breath. Coughing out smoke from his lungs, the boy's chest heaved, fighting for air. But his eyes stayed closed and he was unresponsive when Harry frantically begged, "*Sebastian, wake up. You have to wake up!*"

Struggling to collect his thoughts, Harry knew that he had to get Sebastian off the train as soon as he could. He'd kept a secret from him when they emailed Sebastian's friend to have him change the rails the train would travel on. Harry knew about the dead end coming closer.

***

Over the incessant droning of the chopper blades, the pilot called out, "Calgary command, this is Canadian Air Rescue 15. Over."

"Calgary command, over," he heard a voice through his headphones.

"We have the runaway train in sight, heading south of Canmore toward Columbia Ravine. Estimating time if impact as ten minutes. Over."

"Confirm condition of train. Over."

"Several boxcars along with the engine appear fire-damaged and—*confirming survivors.* Repeat, we have survivors. Over."

"Status of survivors. Over."

Spying through binoculars, the co-pilot responded, "Two males are clinging to the roof of one boxcar. One appears unresponsive. Over."

"Initiate rescue procedure. Over," Calgary command authorized.

Reporting further, the pilot cautioned, "Confirming significant replicate debris near the survivors. Calgary command, please advise. Over."

After a long pause, the pilot repeated, "Calgary command, please advise. Over."

"Abort, risk too great. Over," Calgary command responded.

"Those are humans down there. I'm sure of it," the co-pilot said, anxiously looking to the pilot.

Sighing, the pilot affirmed, "Calgary command, mission—aborted. Over."

"One of them is a kid," the co-pilot revealed. "Maybe he's the other's son."

Saying nothing, the pilot veered the chopper away. "Calgary command, Canadian Air Rescue 15 returning to base. Out." Turning to his co-pilot, he spoke while reaching out, "Dan, listen—."

"*Don't,*" the co-pilot angrily interrupted, pulling away.

***

"Hey, kiddo, you have to wake up," Sebastian heard his dad say.

Sebastian wanted to speak but his lips stung and the burning sensation down his throat and through his nose kept him from barely breathing. Fully exhausted and aching from head-to-toe, he just wanted to sleep. He just wanted everything to be over. Knowing that it really wasn't his dad talking to him made things seem worse.

"Sebastian, it's Scotty," he then heard. "You're one of the smartest guys I've ever met. If anyone can survive this, it's you. Think of all this as a program. Look for the crumbs—or find the backdoor. There's always a back door."

He wanted to laugh at how ridiculous Scotty's comment about the backdoor seemed, but he couldn't. One doesn't just find the exit on a high-speed runaway train. The only real option is to jump and most likely die. Maybe that was the answer. *Maybe I'm surrounded by backdoors,* Sebastian thought. *If I only had the strength to jump off.*

"Listen to me. You—*need—to—get—up,*" his dad's voice returned, sounding angry this time. "You need to try," he reasoned. "I'm waiting for you. All you have to do is wake up. *Please,*" his dad begged. "I can't fail you again."

You didn't fail me, Dad, Sebastian thought. *You've never failed me.*

***

The glimmer of hope Harry had felt in watching the approach of the rescue helicopter vanished when it abruptly turned away. Left with wondering why they'd been abandoned, the answer came clear when one of the thought-to-be-damaged replicates began crawling toward them. Easing Sebastian from his lap, Harry unsteadily stood up, glaring at the replicate. "I'm gonna put an end to you," he mumbled, staggering toward it. And when nearing it, he noticed how two others began moving.

Now concerned there might be other undamaged or partially damaged replicates, Harry stepped back toward Sebastian. Returning to him, he lifted his limp body, dragging him to the edge of the boxcar. But before attempting a leap to the next one, he spotted the remains of a replicate emerging from the far end of the next boxcar. With his heart sinking in his chest, he slumped down to his knees, still holding Sebastian close. "You gotta wake up. We're in pretty deep, here."

"*I'm—I'm—awake,*" Sebastian faintly mumbled, causing Harry to burst out laughing with relief.

Hugging him tighter, Harry asked, "Do you trust me?"

"*Yeah, Dad, I trust you,*" Sebastian uttered, confusing Harry for only a moment and then making him smile.

Kissing his forehead, Harry whispered, "Goodbye, son," and then tossed him off the train.

Chapter Fourteen

Absentmindedly gazing out toward a fog bank hovering over San Francisco Bay, Lexia's attention was pulled away by a call from her secretary. "Yes, Fiona."

"General Reddinger is here, requesting to speak directly to you regarding an urgent matter."

Crookedly raising her eyebrows, Lexia responded, "Send the general in."

Swiveling her chair away from the windows, Lexia stood up as her office door opened. "Good afternoon, general. To what do I owe this unexpected pleasure?"

Marching toward her desk, General Jaclyn Reddinger ignored Lexia's question and instead directly addressed her reason for being there. "We can dispense with the pleasantries. And no, before you ask, I'm not interested in a cappuccino or espresso—or even a damn cup of coffee."

"Of—course," Lexia uttered, knowing full well that the black female general standing before her, once more was all business.

"Something's happened in Canada," the general revealed. "The high-speed train transporting advanced replicate soldiers to the Yukon was destroyed in Alberta."

"How?"

"When traveling through an area engulfed in wildfires, it was diverted to a dead-end track leading south toward the Montana border. Everything was a total loss."

"And why would the Canadian government divert a high-speed train to tracks leading to a dead end," Lexia cautiously asked.

"Apparently their transit authority database was hacked."

"Do we know the perpetrator of their system?"

"Nothing can be confirmed at this time. Our most credible lead is a traced suspicious email path reaching as far as Montreal, but the trail there has grown cold."

"I see," Lexia quietly responded while thinking back to a recent conversation with someone in Montreal.

"Security cameras at the train shipping yards captured images of two vagrants seen wandering on the grounds. You should have received an email from my administrative assistant with these images."

Returning to her desk, Lexia's hand glided over her computer keyboard, typing in her password to access her email. Seeing the message referred to by the general, Lexia pulled up the email and opened the attached file. An unfamiliar man's image first appeared, looking as if a disheveled ringmaster from a circus. Lexia swallowed hard as she reviewed the next image, attempting to hide her shock at seeing a young man familiar to her.

"Do you recognize either of them," the general asked, closely watching her for any reaction.

Lexia lied, casually commenting, "A presumably mentally ill drifter and a teen runaway can hardly be considered suspects." Stepping away from her desk, she continued, "We will, of course, replenish the supply of replicate soldiers at no expense to the government. It will, however take several weeks in establishing the logistics of delivery."

"*Days*, possibly. *Weeks,* out of the question," General Reddinger not-so-politely responded to Lexia's timeline. Moving next to Lexia, she added, "From one bitch to another, make it happen *quickly*—before I lose what little patience I have left with you."

***

Feeling something hot pelt against his face, Sebastian opened his eyes, seeing a grey mist hovering heavily in the air. Both near and far stood the ghostly trunks of trees scorched of their greenery, seeming more like grave markers than the remnants of a once sprawling forest. Drops of dark rain began falling, causing steam to rise from the heated ash-covered ground. Forcing his dried lips apart, Sebastian tried tasting the raindrops to quench his thirst but grimaced at their bitter flavor.

Rolling to his side, pain radiated from his head to his feet. Each shallow breath caused his chest to ache. Surprisingly, with slight movements made, he thought he hadn't broken any bones, but was certain that everything was bruised. Judging by the thickness of the ash under him, Sebastian guessed that it had cushioned his fall when landing on it.

The light rain shower intensified, drenching his dirty face. He'd hoped it would at least cool him, yet it only made him feel warmer, as if laying in a sauna. Enveloped with this heat from both the ground and rain, he glanced down at his blackened body and wondered how he would ever find the strength to stand. A thought crossed his mind to just lay there and fall asleep, maybe never wake up. After all, what was there to stay awake for?

And what about Harry, what happened to him? Maybe he jumped off the train and was crawling around somewhere out there, searching for him. But the train was speeding so fast. If Harry did jump off, he could be anywhere. With a shallow exhale full of regret, Sebastian knew he didn't have the strength to find him. Harry was gone, just like his dad.

Sebastian snuggled his face against the heated ash, acting as his pillow. Closing his eyes, he wondered what his life in Alaska would have been like had he made it there. Would his dad be waiting for him? Remembering his escape from Sidney's house in Montreal, he figured the answer would be no. No one would be there, ready to greet him. So why even bother going? Too tired, aching worse than ever before, all he wanted to do was sleep—and hopefully *not* dream. But soon he realized he couldn't even do this.

Hearing the distant barking of a dog reminded him of Silas. He tried smiling, thinking that Silas had tracked his scent all the way here. That would be nice, having the dog with him again. This seemed like a dream he could let himself enjoy. But some dreams don't stay sweet. The echoing of a gun being fired lured him back to reality.

So at least one replicate had survived falling from the train and remained undamaged enough to fire its weapon. But what was it firing at? Possibly a malfunction of its software implant caused it to randomly discharge its weapon. With luck, maybe it will point the gun to its own head and pull the trigger.

After laying there for a while, listening to the continuing shots fired, Sebastian realized that the dog's barking hadn't stopped. It sounded much closer now. Opening his eyes, he noticed how the rain was more like mist, evaporating before reaching the ground. The light mist had changed to a dense fog, shrouding almost everything from view with the exception of one bare tree trunk. As he continued looking the silhouette of a figure emerged from behind it. What looked like a weapon lowered in its grasp, pointing toward him. Sebastian held his breath while strangely flooded with relief. It was over.

An explosion of sparks eerily lit the fog as the figure dropped to the ground following a deafening blast of gunfire. Sebastian winced with throbbing pain in his ears from hearing this so close. Attempting to catch his breath, he then froze when a pure white dog, a husky he thought, wandered near him, whimpering as its paws pranced.

Sebastian heard a man's voice call out, "What did you find, Kodiak?" A minute later, Sebastian saw a man, wearing a red rescue-type uniform, kneel down in front of him. "You are one lucky kid. Do you know that?" Reaching over to touch his head, the man continued, "I need you to hold on. I'm gonna get you to a hospital as soon as I can. Stay with me, pal." Turning to the dog, the man commanded, "Stay." The dog lay on its belly, panting and keeping its eyes on Sebastian as the man jogged away.

Slowly reaching his quaking arm out, Sebastian's fingers lightly ran through the dog's soft fur. Tilting its head to the side, the dog licked his hand with its tail wagging excitedly. "*Good boy*," he whispered to it, hearing a vehicle pulling up.

Appearing again before him, the man knelt on one knee while reaching his arms out. "I'm sorry if this hurts. I'm gonna carry you to my jeep. The hospital is about an hour away, but we'll get there in twenty minutes because I drive fast," he said, grinning.

Feeling light-headed and wanting to throw up, Sebastian closed his eyes while being carried. Once resting on the passenger seat, the man wrapped a blanket around him and then held a bottle of water to his lips. "Here, you need to drink this." Only a little made it to his throat as the rest dripped down his chin.

"*My friend is somewhere out there. I need to find him*," Sebastian breathlessly whispered.

With a distressed look on his face, the man responded, "I think I know who you're talking about. He didn't make it off the train. I'm sorry." Looking directly to him, the man continued, "I found a male human body surrounded by replicates at the crash site, yesterday."

"*Yesterday?*" Sebastian confusingly echoed.

"Yeah, pal. The train you were riding on crashed into a concrete barrier just before reaching the Columbia Ravine yesterday afternoon. The whole thing was destroyed. The only human casualty found near the wreckage was a man wearing a circus ringmaster's jacket. Was he your friend?"

Swallowing hard and closing his eyes, Sebastian answered, "Yeah."

Seemingly unknowing in what else to say about his friend, the man tucked the blanket tighter around Sebastian. Reaching around him with the seatbelt, the man commented, "You need this on. The locks on this old piece of junk don't work. I'm sure you'd rather not fall out," he said with a grin before closing his door. Then getting in, with the dog sitting between them, the man floored the gas pedal, speeding away down what might have been an old logging road before the wildfire.

Glancing out his window, through the now lifting fog, Sebastian saw several replicates lying motionless on the ground. *"How—did you find me?"* he faintly asked.

"I was the co-pilot in a helicopter flying over the wildfire yesterday. We saw the train speeding through it and followed it to see where it was heading. Calgary Command received an anonymous tip about the train being diverted to a dead-end track. No one was able to stop it. Anyway, as we were flying over it, I spotted you and your friend on one of the boxcars. I wanted to try to rescue you both then, but didn't out of fear you were both replicates."

Turning his head toward the man, Sebastian asked, "Do I look like a replicate?"

Somewhat grinning, the man answered, "No, pal. Not even yesterday did you look like one." Sighing, he continued, "But Calgary didn't see what we saw and the pilot refused to disobey a direct command."

Thinking for a moment, Sebastian then commented, "They wanted the train to be destroyed and the replicates with it."

"Yes."

"But you came back."

"Yes. We had to be sure that the replicates were destroyed. That's when we found your friend."

"What made you come looking for me?"

"You're somebody's son. I couldn't just leave you out there alone. I wanted to make sure I did everything I could to get you home."

"How did you find me?"

A moment passed before the man answered, "Well, as it turns out, it wasn't really hard. You see those replicates out there? They were hunting you."

Chapter Fifteen

Awakening tired and sore, he focused his sight on the blades of a ceiling fan rotating slowly overhead. Feeling dizzy he closed his eyes, taking a couple of deep breaths, which hurt. Trying to sit up, Sebastian quickly changed his mind and eased back down onto the firm bed under him, running a hand over his bandaged ribs. Tilting his head forward, he saw his left knee wrapped with another bandage and a black leg brace on his right leg, from his knee to his ankle. What he also saw was the dimly lit, cheap-looking hotel room surrounding him. Having been told he'd be taken to a hospital by the man who rescued him, Sebastian had no idea how he ended up here.

Unsure of the time of day due to the window blinds being drawn, he glanced over to the nightstand, seeing a digital clock blinking the number twelve and the television remote just within reach. Turning it on loud enough to just barely hear the volume, he scrolled through the channels to find anything confirming the hour. The local weather report for Calgary showed the time as a few minutes before eight in the evening.

Just when turning the television off, someone unlocked the hotel room's door. As it opened, Sebastian saw the man who'd rescued him walk through the door, carrying two department store bags in his hands. "Nice to see you awake," the man greeted with a smile.

"This doesn't look like the hospital room you promised," Sebastian commented as the man turned on the table lamp across the room.

"Oh, you were there for a couple days," he answered. "Heavily sedated," he added. "I'd be surprised if you remembered any of it."

"I don't."

"That's probably a good thing."

"Why do you say that?"

Sitting on the edge of the bed, the man lightly patted Sebastian's leg brace. "You my friend have a very important admirer. Someone named *Lexia*."

Attempting to stay calm, Sebastian asked, "How does she know I'm here?"

"Well, being that you weren't carrying any identification, except your friend's wallet, the hospital took a picture of you and conducted an internet search of runaway kids. They found a notification for a missing American teen, matching your picture from San Francisco. You sure get around, Sebastian," he finished, looking impressed.

"Well, now you know my name. What's yours?"

"Dan Cramer, nice to meet you," he answered, extending his hand to Sebastian.

"Where are we?"

"The Royal Maple Hotel, near the airport."

"Why are we here?"

Appearing lost in thought, Dan answered, "After they found out who you are, things got *strange* at the hospital, and away from it. Just out of the blue, a security guard began hanging out near your door, watching the doctors and nurses come and go, and me also. Then someone followed me home one night. A neighbor-friend of mine was questioned about me. So I helped you get away from there and brought you here."

"Why are you helping me?"

"I don't know. You seem like a nice kid," Dan responded. Although his tone sounded sincere, the fact that he looked away when saying this seemed off. He also appeared nervous, which he tried to hide.

Acting okay with his answer, Sebastian changed the subject. "I need a shower." Then looking under the sheet, he added, "And some clothes."

Smirking, Dan pulled his bags up onto the bed. "Great minds must think alike. I bought you some t-shirts, two pairs of jeans, socks, boxers, sneakers, and a jacket."

"Wow. Thanks!"

"No problem, my friend. As for the shower, I'm not the type to scrub a guy's back."

"And I appreciate that," Sebastian remarked.

"I can help you with the bandages and your leg brace," Dan offered.

"No, I can handle them."

"Are you hungry?"

"Starving. You didn't by chance buy me a cheeseburger, did you?"

Laughing, Dan answered, "No, but there's a restaurant across the street. Do you want fries with that?"

"Sounds like you worked there before," Sebastian sarcastically joked.

Continuing to laugh, Dan replied, "No, I worked for some white-haired guy pushing chicken. I'll be back in about ten minutes," he said as he walked out the door.

Grabbing the clothes off the bed, Sebastian noticed Harry's wallet sitting on the desk next to the television. Taking it with him, he walked into the bathroom, closing and locking the door behind him. Seeing a long narrow window in the shower stall, he guessed he was skinny enough to slip through it but he'd need something to stand on. Stepping back out into the main room, he retrieved the desk chair and once more closed and locked the door behind him.

After getting dressed, stopping twice when feeling lightheaded, he climbed the chair and opened the window, which fortunately had a screen that could easily be yanked off. Searching out, he noticed the room was on the ground floor. Knowing he'd dropped from fences much taller than the window, he knew he's have no problem getting out.

Halfway through climbing out the window, Sebastian reached over, turning on the shower. When ready to slip the rest of the way out, he heard Dan return. Knocking on the bathroom door, Dan called, "You almost done? Your food's gonna get cold."

"I'll be out in a minute," Sebastian answered, not a lie considering he really *would* be out in a minute, just not where Dan expected. And just before finishing his escape, he heard a loud knock on the outer door. Holding still for a moment, Sebastian heard Dan talking to someone. Although he couldn't tell who he was talking to, he heard Dan say, "Yeah, he's in the bathroom" and "I did what you told me to."

Dropping down to the ground, Sebastian exhaled his breath, wincing in pain from all over his body. Quickly looking around, he staggered down the alley and around the corner. Seeing no place close for hiding, when noticing Dan's four-door jeep at the far edge of the parking lot, he remembered that the locks didn't work. Maybe he could slip in and hide there until he could think of something better?

Sneaking around several other parked vehicles, Sebastian believed he hadn't been seen as he approached and then snuck in the back seat of Dan's jeep. Finding the blanket he'd been wrapped in when rescued, he covered most of himself with it while peering out through the front seats, looking at the hotel. A minute later, Dan stepped out of the hotel room, stuffing an envelope into his pocket while walking away.

Seeing him coming, Sebastian pulled the blanket the rest of the way over his head, completely hiding his body from sight. Holding his breath when feeling the door open,

Sebastian's ears only heard the thunderous sound of what he thought was a jet overhead, either taking off or landing. But by the time the jet had passed, with the echoes of its engines growing softer, Sebastian still hadn't felt the car door close. Everything was quiet, almost as if too quite.

Peeking out from under the blanket, Sebastian noticed the jeep's interior light on, meaning the door hadn't closed. Sitting further up and cautiously leaning forward, he saw that the hotel room's door was left wide open with the inside dark. Glancing to his left he saw Dan lying on the pavement. Crawling up between the front seats, Sebastian discovered why.

Covered with blood, a bullet hole in Dan's forehead revealed that he'd been murdered. Somehow Sebastian thought he was the reason for this. Remembering what he had overheard and the envelope he saw Dan stuffing in his pocket and how strange he seemed in the hotel room, Sebastian guessed that his rescuer might have taken a bribe to turn him over to Lexia, or men she had working for her. And once it was discovered that he'd run away, Dan paid the price for failing to deliver him. Looking down at his dead body, Sebastian felt torn between feeling sad and relieved.

Strangely entranced by staring at Dan's dead body, other than the blood seeping from the bullet hole he looked like the passed out replicate guard on the train. Remembering how all other replicates acted when he'd been near them left him wondering if Harry had told him the truth. Was the guard on the train human? Sebastian now believed so.

Knowing he needed to get as far away as possible, Sebastian climbed out of Dan's jeep, stepping over his body. It occurred to him to find his keys and drive away, although he'd never driven anything before. He quickly decided against this, hoping that Dan's murder would appear as a simple robbery to the police. He could slip away unnoticed, and hopefully unfollowed in getting out of Calgary.

Realizing he needed some money, Sebastian wearily glanced around, fearful of someone watching as he kneeled down to find Dan's wallet. He wasn't surprised in discovering that the envelope Dan had received was gone. But while pulling some loose change from one pocket, he was surprised to find a small piece of paper with only a phone number written on it. And when finally pulling his wallet out of his back pocket, Sebastian did, in fact, feel sad for him when seeing a picture of Dan and a pretty woman, guessing she might be his wife or girlfriend. Taking what money he had, Sebastian whispered, "I'm sorry."

A short while later, when approaching a fast food restaurant, he noticed a public telephone. Curiosity overwhelmed him. He dropped several coins in the slot and waited to hear the dial tone. Frustrated by the tremor coursing through his hand, pressing the numbers on the dial pad proved difficult. Holding his breath, he waited to hear the answer on the other end.

"Hello," a familiar female voice greeted. Unnerved and not knowing what to say, he was about to hang up when she said, "Sebastian, is that you?"

"I just want to be left alone," he blurted out.

"You know I can't do that. There's too much at stake." With further words choked in his throat, Sebastian nearly broke down when she asked, "Where is your father?"

"I don't know," he uttered, growing confused and lightheaded.

"I could help you find him."

Sebastian hung up. Needing to get as far away as he could he stopped an elderly man who was walking by and asked, "Excuse me sir, is there a truck stop nearby?"

"About two or three miles down the road," the man replied.

"Thanks."

Hindered by the pain radiating throughout his body, he slowly walked away, arriving at a rather large truck stop what seemed like an eternity later. Glancing about at the large semis both coming and going, he stepped over to one who caught his eye, asking the driver, "Excuse me. I was hoping to catch a ride with you out of town."

"Sure, where you headed?"

Having thought about this question almost the entire time while walking here, Sebastian answered, "Edmonton, or as close to it as I can get."

"You're in luck. I'm headed just north of there. Hop in."

Once inside, the driver commented, "I know it's none of my business, but a nice-looking boy like you shouldn't be out this late, especially trying to hitch a ride with a stranger."

"I need to get home quick," Sebastian lied. "Anyway, I trust you."

Chuckling, the driver, a rather burly, older, bearded man, remarked, "Yeah, I must really look like a nice guy."

Pointing to something hanging off the dashboard, Sebastian revealed, "Actually, it's your picture of Jesus that makes me trust you. That and your cross earing and necklace."

"The lord will provide," the driver happily offered, leaving Sebastian wondering for a moment if the driver's words were true.

Glancing out the window, in just wanting some light conversation, Sebastian asked, "What time is it?"

Checking his wristwatch, the driver answered, "Close to midnight."

Chapter Sixteen

Hobbling down the tree-lined street of what seemed like a middle-class neighborhood, Sebastian hoped he wasn't drawing too much attention to himself. The early afternoon sun filtered down through shade trees which shivered in comfortable gusts. Checking the house numbers, he knew he was getting closer. Finally reaching the address on Harry's military identification card, he stood out in front of the nice looking two-story white house with well-tended shrubs and flowers. Remembering Harry and how he appeared, this place didn't seem anything like where he should have been from. But Sebastian understood how people can be changed by experiencing war and death, causing them to become disconnected with the life they used to lead.

Separated from the front yard by a white picket fence, Sebastian opened the gate and walked up the river stone sidewalk to the front door. He held still, not having any idea what to say when the door opened. Sighing deeply, feeling unable to go through with this, Sebastian turned around to leave. But just before reaching the gate, his steps were halted by the voice of a woman speaking behind him. "May I help you?"

Turning around and swallowing hard, Sebastian stood there before Harry's wife, Elaine. Although the picture of Harry and his family had been taken years ago, his wife had maintained her pretty, youthful appearance. Believing he couldn't pull off lying about Harry, from his pocket, Sebastian pulled out his picture and handed it to her. "I think Harry wanted you to have this."

Clearly alarmed by what he said, she hesitated taking the picture from him, and when doing so began to cry while covering her mouth with her hand. *"Please, come inside,"* she begged.

Following her into the house, they passed through a comfortably furnished living room with a fireplace and on to the kitchen. From an upper cabinet, she pulled out a bottle of wine, popping off the cork and drinking straight from the bottle. Then taking a moment in seeming to collect her thoughts, she found a glass, filling it to the brim.

"I never meant to upset you," Sebastian quietly offered.

Closing her eyes, she whispered, "It's all right. I knew this moment could happen someday. I just don't know how anyone prepares for it." Before he could say anything else, she asked, "When? Where?"

"About a week ago, south of Calgary."

"So close," she commented before gulping some of her wine. "Did he suffer?"

"I don't think so, at least I hope not. I was with him, just before the end."

Taking notice of his trembling hands and how he seemed to be in pain when moving, Elaine asked, "Did he hurt you?"

"No, he saved me." Seeing her watching his hands, he revealed, "I have Parkinson's disease."

"I'm sorry. I—."

"It's okay. It's just something I live with." She smiled kindly to him, appearing to understand.

Seeming to hesitate, she then asked, "How was he?"

Thinking over this, Sebastian offered, "He seemed at peace with his life."

Both were then startled when the sliding door leading to the back deck opened and in stepped Harry. "Well, *hi* there! Who are you?" He casually asked, walking passed his wife.

Unable to utter a word, Sebastian just stared at him, as if looking at a ghost. Barefoot and dressed in black cargo shorts and a white polo shirt, the muscular-bodied, clean-shaven Harry getting a drink of water from the refrigerator appeared completely different from the skinny, bearded Harry he knew from the train.

"This is Tommy, my friend Cara's son," Elaine quickly lied. "He stopped by so I can answer a few computer questions for him."

"Well, don't let me interrupt you," Harry answered. Before stepping back outside, he said, "The hot dogs are almost ready. Tommy, can you stay for lunch?"

Again, coming to his rescue, Elaine answered, "No, his mom is expecting him home in a little while."

"Too bad. Anyway, nice to meet you," Harry said, smiling and then leaving them alone.

"I can explain," Elaine offered. Motioning for him to sit down, Elaine took her seat at the table and waited for Sebastian to sit. "I didn't want our sons to grow up without a father," she blankly commented while studying her glass of wine. "When Harry returned from Iran, there was something damaged inside him, something no one was able to fix. He tried counseling and medications, but he was afraid that through his anger and fits of delusions he might hurt me and our sons, so he left."

"Then who is that?"

"I'm a professor of advanced computer programming at a university here in Edmonton. We had received several replicates, captured by the Canadian military, for educational study. One lonely night when working late here at home, a thought occurred to me that I had the ability and resources to do something *unthinkable*."

"So you changed the programming in one of the replicates," Sebastian interrupted. Just like *Frankenstein* you created—."

"My husband," she stopped him from saying 'a monster'. "By installing new data with everything I could remember about him, soon enough he responded and acted just as Harry would have. Other, cosmetic technology, allowed me to alter the replicate's appearance so that it even resembled Harry."

"How have you kept this secret from your sons? Don't they notice that he's different?"

"I told them a half-truth, that his time in the military changed him. It didn't take long for them to accept the subtle differences in him. To them, he's a loving, devoted father. They adore him."

"And what about you?"

Appearing noticeably emotional, Elaine answered, "I've learned to appreciate the monster I've created."

"But not love it, like they do."

"No. Never."

"What if Harry came home and found out what you'd done?"

"He *did* come home and he saw everything." Gulping the rest of her wine, as if willing it to give her courage, Elaine continued, "It was just this past Christmas, we were all sitting around the tree opening our presents, just one happy family. After the boys had gone to bed that night, he knocked on the door. Harry told me he'd spent the whole day outside in the bitter cold, spying through the window as we moved from one holiday ritual to the next." Brushing some tears aside, she added, "He wasn't angry. He told me he loved me and our sons, and he promised not to come back to spoil things for us."

"I don't understand. He came home. How could you just let him leave?" Bursting in tears, Elaine offered no words of response for his question.

Glancing out the window, he watched as the replicate Harry tossed a football with one of his sons, seeing nothing but happiness on both their faces.

Remembering the short amount of time he'd spent with his dad at the lighthouse, he understood how her son felt and knew he couldn't damage something like that. Standing up, Sebastian looked down at her. "I won't tell anyone your secret. I promise."

"Thank you," she responded, clearly anxious. As he turned to leave, she asked, "Is there anything I can do for you?"

"No."

"Where will you go from here?"

"Alaska, maybe. I don't know."

***

Ten days later

Feeling as if his head would explode, Scotty stopping working on his advanced calculus equations. Rubbing his temples while silently cursing his teacher over her sadistic homework assignment, he closed his textbook. "I need some water and some air," he mumbled to himself, standing up at his table in the school resource center.

Wandering the hallway to the restroom, after coming out he found the water fountain and then returned, handing the hall pass back to the librarian. Wanting not to continue his homework, Scotty walked over to the classical literature section, scanning the book titles with little interest in selecting one to read, with an exception. From the shelf he withdrew a familiar book, holding it in his hands.

"Have you read that before?" Mister Dominic quietly asked, startling him from the trance the book's cover held over him.

"No, a friend gave me a copy but I haven't read it yet."

"*Brave New World* is a fascinating novel. You really should find the time to read it," Mister Dominic urged before being pulled away to scold some students for loud talking.

Having no more reasons to delay returning to his homework, Scotty sat down and opened his textbook, taking time in finding the required page. Then glancing at his notebook, he dropped his mechanical pencil when seeing the impossible. Someone had finished his homework, providing both the answers and showing the work for each equation. Glancing at the students sitting at tables near his, Scotty felt sure none of them could have completed his assignment in the short amount of time he was away. And with him being the smartest kid in school, if he struggled with the equations, then they were having a far worse time with them. Pulling his calculator close to him, he found a note when opening the leather cover.

Scotty,

I'm not sure why you were having such trouble with this homework. I thought it was pretty easy. Oh, by the way, I like your Tron t-shirt. Great old movie.

S.

Spinning around with his heart in his throat, Scotty stood up, frantically searching around the resource center for any traces of Sebastian, but finding none.

***

Spying out from behind the closed concession stand, Sebastian watched Nikki sitting by herself on the bleachers. Upon arriving in Sea Bridge just shortly after daybreak, as he was walking through town passed the high school, he unexpectedly saw Abdul dropping off Scotty and Nikki. Never imagining seeing them again, his first thought was to rush up to them, letting them know he was alive. But with all that had happened to him, his mind pushed his impulse to be seen aside, choosing instead to be more cautious. He spent the day shadowing them both while trying to stay inconspicuous to the other students and teachers. At times he blended in, but for the most part he remained hidden.

But now the urge to reveal himself to Nikki won out over his nervousness. Stepping out from his hiding place and walking toward her, Sebastian stopped when three girls approached her, sitting down and bursting with laughter and conversation. He wanted their first moment seeing each other to be private, so he backed away, returning to his previous spot hidden behind the concession stand. With their gossiping and banter seemingly endless, he was growing impatient with every passing minute. Then something happened that caught him completely off guard.

Three boys his age, wearing football jerseys and letter jackets, joined the girls. The tallest one, blond-haired and perfect-looking, eased up behind Nikki, wrapping her in his arms. It was obvious she enjoyed the boy's attention. And when she tilted her head enough for him to kiss her Sebastian's heart sank. Swallowing hard while leaning his head against the concession stand, Sebastian whispered, "She forgot about me." Heartbroken and unwilling to watch further, he quietly backed away, turning then to leave and not looking back.

Chapter Seventeen

Absently watching the brilliant orange-colored sky through the partial canopy of leaves overhanging the roadside, Sebastian slowly walked down a lonely road. Having watched Nikki kissing another boy robbed him of the unexpected joy of seeing her and Scotty after arriving in the morning. A thought crossed his mind that maybe he should have run up to them, letting them know that he was there and safe. He knew what Scotty would have thought but what would *her* reaction have been? It was more than obvious that she and the boy are a couple. Was it better to have found out by seeing them together as he did? Would she have told him later if he'd tried to kiss her? Sighing heavily, he imagined the aching disappointment inside him would eventually go away. At least he hoped it would.

He'd spent the past few hours walking around town, most of it near the docks. Seeing the fishing trawlers returning from a long day at sea, he watched the men walk home, probably to families waiting for them. What would it be like to walk in the door and hear someone say how happy they are that you're home? Having never experienced anything like that, Sebastian couldn't even imagine how that might seem.

Spotting several deer crossing further ahead, Sebastian tried focusing on them instead of feeling sorry for himself. The forest lining the road, the occasional views of the ocean and distant mountains was everything he thought of when deciding to come to Alaska. A quiet, out-of-the-way place in this world might just be where he could hide for a while. But after thinking this, headlight reflections on a nearby road sign reminded him he wasn't alone.

Hearing a vehicle skidding to a stop off the side of the road behind him caused Sebastian to shudder with fear. Halting his steps when noticing the engine turning off and the car door opening, he tried calmly counting to ten before turning around. And when reaching the number nine, a hand firmly gripping his shoulder robbed him of his breath. Unable to move, he closed his eyes when sensing the person stepping in front of him.

"I know someone who misses you very much," he heard a man's familiar voice say.

Opening his eyes, Abdul's beaming expression appeared. Exhaling his relief, Sebastian was dragged into Abdul's strong, seemingly endless embrace, even being slightly lifted into the air. With no words passing between them, Sebastian allowed himself to relax, knowing he was safe. Then hearing words making him want to cry, Abdul whispered in his ear, "It's time to come home."

Taking a step back, Sebastian asked, "How did you know it was me?"

Shaking his head, Abdul replied, "I don't know. I can't explain it but I *knew*—I just had to stop." Being pulled back into his embrace, Sebastian breathed easy in feeling safe.

With Abdul keeping his arm draped across his shoulders, Scotty's dad let him to his jeep and opened the door for him. Once both were seated, Abdul started the engine and drove off, repeatedly glancing over with a warm grin.

***

A short while later, after traveling down a winding, secluded driveway, Abdul parked his jeep in front of a two-story modern steel and stone house, having a breathtaking scenic water view. A few of the floor-to-ceiling glass windows shone the architectural details of the lighted interior.

"Wow! It's beautiful," Sebastian uttered.

"That is my house," Abdul proudly exclaimed. A moment later, hearing Scotty and Nikki arguing inside, he added with a sigh, "And that would be my children."

A laugh escaping him, Sebastian asked, "Do they argue like that all the time?"

"Ask me when they *don't*. That would be an easier question to answer," Abdul responded.

"Maybe I could stop them from killing each other," Sebastian suggested.

"Possibly later, but right now it's time for you to go home." Motioning toward a trail leading into some trees, Abdul encouraged him, "Go on, just down the path." As Sebastian stepped in that direction, both heard Xavier yelling over Nikki and Scotty's voices. "I hope he made brownies, otherwise I'll be guzzling chocolate sauce straight from the bottle," Abdul remarked, causing both of them to smile. "Stay on the path and don't get lost. I'll see you later my friend," he added while walking toward his house.

Feeling a sense of relief in knowing his friends were so close, Sebastian wasn't afraid to walk down the stone trail alone. Hearing the rustle of leaves overhead being disturbed by gentle evening breezes further offered peacefulness, relaxing him with each step. Emerging through the trees he saw another modern house before him. This one, somewhat larger than Abdul's, also appeared to be constructed of steel and stone. But what he found different about this house was how it floated on the water, rather than being built on shore. The floor-to-ceiling windows were all dark, with exception of a dim light illuminating the top of a spiral metal staircase in the home's center.

Stopping for a moment, looking upon both the house and the moon's fluid reflection on the water, Sebastian wondered if he could finally call this place home. That's what he hoped, but things he'd wanted in the past never seemed to last very long. Maybe this time would be different.

Crossing a metal bridge over to the house's wrap-around deck, Sebastian heard the tranquil impact of the remnants of waves colliding with the rocks lining the beach. The haunting call of whales somewhere nearby in the ocean reminded him of their melody from when he and his dad were at the lighthouse. It seemed as though a lifetime had passed since being there.

Looking through the windows, Sebastian saw the light from a digital clock reflecting of polished surfaces in the kitchen. He then noticed low burning flames in a fireplace, leading him to wonder if someone else might be here. The sound of splashing coming from around the other side of the house furthered his suspicion of not being alone.

Cautiously treading across the deck to the other side of the house, the sight of his dad standing there in light cast off from an outdoor fireplace brought him to a halt. Seeming to become aware of a presence, his dad turned toward him. Gripping a black steel post to steady him, Lee's lips and jaw moved, yet no words escaped his throat.

Reeling with the guilt of abandoning him back in Montreal, Sebastian forced out, "I'm sorry I left you behind."

"You don't have anything to be sorry about," his dad breathlessly corrected him.

"Are you okay?" Sebastian quietly asked.

"I wasn't until now," Lee choked out. "I should be the one asking that."

"I'm tired," Sebastian uttered. "Everything hurts."

Slowly stepping toward him, "You look like hell," making Sebastian smile.

With his smile quickly fading, Sebastian burst out, "Dad, I don't want to run anymore. I don't want to hide. I can't do this again."

"I know. I'm so sorry, kiddo. You won't ever have to again. I promise. You're home; you're safe." Then walking over to him, Lee gently brushed the back of his hand against Sebastian's cheek before holding him tight. "I'm so sorry," he softly kept repeating, pulling Sebastian closer to him each time he said it.

Quaking in his dad's arms, Sebastian mumbled, "Sidney injected me with that stuff."

Pulling back to look in his face, Lee responded, "I know."

Struggling to speak, he whispered, "How long— before –I end up—like Lydia."

Cradling his son's face in the palms of his hand, Lee answered, "I won't let that happen." Shifting his eyes, glancing behind Sebastian, he added, "I know something you don't."

"Daddy, I had a nightmare," Sebastian heard Lydia softly say from behind him, sending a chill down his spine.

"Come here princess," Lee said to her, causing Sebastian to look at his dad, completely shocked by his reaction.

Stepping back, with his heart pounding in his chest he watched Lydia approach them, wearing pink pajamas and wiping the sleep from her eyes. Then stopping when seeing him, Lydia smiled. "Hello Sebastian."

Feeling his dad there behind him, he heard him say, "Sidney found a way to help her. She won't hurt you, I promise. Talk to her, it's okay."

But before he could find the courage to, something caught her attention. Pointing toward the sky, Lydia asked, "What is that? It's pretty."

Seeing what drew her interest, Sebastian answered, "It's the Aurora Borealis, the northern lights."

"I like the color," she commented.

Watching her close, there was something gentle and simple about her mannerisms. The spark of childish wonder and innocence shone clearly in her expression. Turning to his dad, before Sebastian could ask, his dad answered his unspoken question. "She has high-functioning autism. It's as if everything cruel inside her has been erased. Sidney was able to refine the drugs and alter the dosage to help her."

"And what about me?"

Sighing, Lee explained, "He can't cure your Parkinson's disease but he can lessen the severity of your symptoms. You'll probably need to take medication for the rest of your life. None of it will cause you the side effects that Lydia or the others suffered."

Sebastian stumbled back, stunned when seeing Silas padding around the corner. Vigorously wagging his tale, he bolted over to him, knocking him to his knees and excitedly licking his face. "How?" Sebastian breathlessly uttered.

Grinning, Lee answered, "I went back for him, before coming here. He was still waiting on the other side of the bridge."

"Good boy," Sebastian said, petting his dog.

Then with surprise, Lydia grabbed his hand, "Come on. Watch this with me." Dragging him over to sit down next to her, the awe gripping her stare at the northern lights was clear by how excited she acted. Then abruptly glancing down, she looked at him oddly and then said, "I like how your hand shakes."

Unsure of what else to say, he simply replied, "Thanks."

With her head resting against his shoulder, Lydia asked, "Can we see these lights all the time?"

"I don't know," Sebastian answered. "*Maybe*, but you can only see them after dark."

The End

About Jeffery Martin Botzenhart

I've been waiting for you. So you made it to the end of After Dark. Our friend, Sebastian, certainly isn't having an easy time. But let's not delay in getting to what you want to know about, me. If you've read any of my other stories and survived the boredom of my previous bios you know I'm a small town Ohio boy who grew up wanting to be a writer and an artist, both of which I am. I'm married and have three sons and am a self-professed geek and soccer coach and fan. But you still haven't told me about you. How are you? I see. You're the shy type. Well, I hope you enjoyed this book and look forward to the next. Until then, happy reading!

Social Media Links

Facebook:

https://www.facebook.com/jefferymartinbotzenhartwritingjourney/

Acknowledgements

I would like to thank my brother, John, for his continuing support with my journey as a writer.

If you enjoyed this story, check out these other Solstice Publishing books by Jeffery Martin Botzenhart:

Daybreak – Nightfall Book One

Amidst a world of cyber surveillance and advancing technology of 2035 San Francisco, Sebastian, a teen runaway, innocently access a sophisticated virtual reality program. The breach of this data proves the catalyst in unraveling corporate and government sanctioned deception of the most unimaginable type. And along with his computer hacker friend, Scotty, both are thrust into a dangerous conspiracy, linking them to a source exposing the truth.

https://bookgoodies.com/a/B073SB9BXG

Harvest Fever

A bullied and abused teen boy's plans for escape from a small remote town in Appalachia are hindered by a space alien invasion. Finding everyone in town missing, the aliens begin hunting him. And after being captured, he discovers the unimaginable truth of what's really going on.

https://bookgoodies.com/a//B074JZV44F

Painted Desert

Sung with haunting vocals, a spares fragile melody strummed in the dark on a guitar can be one of many disguises for the lonely. Others, either victims of circumstance or of their own devices stay hidden behind colorful masks and pretty decorations to shield their pain. Yet these masquerades hold flaws for hearts searching to heal, revealing not desolate barren souls as no more than a painted desert, but desert angels waiting to lead the lost to the light.

https://bookgoodies.com/a/B072MZY1FK